Throne of Sin

emily bowie

This book is dedicated to my mom

who always supports my ideas.

Copyright © 2023 by Emily Bowie

All rights reserved.

No portion of this book may be reproduced in any form without written permission from the publisher or author, except as permitted by U.S. copyright law.

Contents

1. Dante — 1
2. Demi — 6
3. Dante — 15
4. Dante — 22
5. Demi — 28
6. Dante — 37
7. Demi — 41
8. Demi — 45
9. Dante — 51
10. Demi — 56
11. Dante — 63
12. Demi — 67
13. Demi — 73
14. Dante — 81
15. Demi — 83
16. Dante — 88
17. Demi — 93
18. Dante — 101
19. Demi — 107

20.	Dante	112
21.	Demi	117
22.	Demi	121
23.	Demi	127
24.	Demi	132
25.	Dante	140
26.	Demi	147
27.	Demi	154
28.	Dante	161
29.	Demi	165
30.	Demi	170
31.	Dante	177
32.	Demi	181
33.	Dante	185
34.	Demi	189
35.	Dante	198
36.	Demi	204
37.	Dante	209
38.	Demi	214
39.	Dante	227
40.	Epilogue	231
41.	Acknowledgments	234
42.	Other books by Emily Bowie	235

Chapter 1

Dante

10 years ago, 19 years old

Screaming has my head snapping up from the kitchen table. I glance at the door, then to my brother Savio. My hands hesitate as I place them on the table to help push myself back.

"Dante..." my mother warns in her sinister voice.

She insists we sit as a family for every meal, even though our family is torn apart and none of us want to put it back together again. She's all about the illusion of family and the power she believes that she holds over us.

My feet shove the chair back and it topples to the ground with a clatter.

"Don't you dare leave this table." My mother wipes her mouth daintily with a white cloth and glares at me.

"She's a big girl who knows how to handle herself, Dante," Savio says under his breath. We both know that's a lie, but he knows what will happen to us if I leave the table.

I glance down at my older brother. He sighs before shoveling another forkful of food into his mouth. We both know I can't conscionably sit still when Demi might need me. Savio tilts his head for me to go, but I hesitate, not wanting another beating. My mother is cunning. It will come when neither of us expects it. I might have seventy pounds on her, but I still refuse to lift a hand to her and she knows it. She uses this to her full advantage.

I leave the table, rushing out of our house and bee-lining it for the one across the street. Demi comes flying out and trips on the stairs, falling onto the hard, cracked concrete. Her father steps out with a black leather belt in his fists, snapping it as he walks closer.

"If you so much as touch her with that, I will strangle you with it in your basement." I step out from the dark shadows, bending down to lift Demi up from the ground. Her cheek is already red and swollen from him hitting her.

"You can't protect her from everything, Dante. She'll have to come home eventually." Her father turns around and slams the door.

"You're only making it worse, Dante." Demi cries into my shoulder.

I hold her tight, one hand sweeping over her long dark locks. Fury ignites in my gut that her father would prey on the weak. He should be out here fighting me instead.

"Come on, we can sit on my roof until he falls asleep." I pull her away, keeping her clutched under my shoulder. She hisses with a limp as she tries to walk. I hold her tighter, taking as much pressure off her leg as I can, and guide her across the street.

"Maybe he'll drink too much and not remember tonight." She hiccups between her soft sobs.

I bend down and pick her up, bridal style, because her limp tells me she's in more pain that she's willing to let on.

"I can walk." She leans her head on my chest, no real fight in her. Damn if it doesn't feel great. I would burn our world down for this girl.

"He won't hurt you again," I vow, my voice fierce as I think of a plan to retaliate. My arms hold her tighter as I consider all the horrible ways I could exact my vengeance for every mark he's ever left on her.

"Don't be making promises you can't keep," she scolds.

I glance down and find her eyes full of fear and uncertainty, the hope of me taking her problem away too big of a thing for her to grasp. I get it. It hurts more when you give a shit and things go sideways. That's been my whole fucking life.

I lick my lips, hating this feeling of inadequacy. I've never excelled at anything. Savio is the fighter in our family and I'm the one with no talents.

I cross the street, walking to the side of the house closest to my bedroom.

"Hold on to my back." I easily maneuver her from my front to my back before I climb up the hidden ladder. It's the easiest way to come and go from my household.

The shingles dig into my palms as I climb onto the roof and set Demi down. I wish I could offer her an ice pack or something to help with the pain. Instead, I sit beside her, my legs stretched out, her body leaning into me as her arms hug her knees to her chest.

"We could run away, leave this hellhole," I suggest. She's the only reason I've stayed this long, anyway. Savio and I have two older brothers, maybe one of them could take us in.

"We could live off the fish in the sea and have a little beach hut," she replies with our typical fantasy talk. It helps to forget our roots while knowing we're never getting out of here. No one ever does.

"I would hunt by day." *Make love to you by night.* I wish I was brave enough to say the last bit out loud.

"I would make us a home. Not a house but, you know...that feeling you get when you're around the right person." I wrap my arm around her and press a kiss to the side of her head. A comfortable silence washes over us as we look up into the star-filled night.

"Jameson asked me out today." And just like that, the comfortable, familiar peace we'd begun to slip into shatters.

My veins turn to ice, and I stiffen automatically. I release her shoulders and turn to look at her. "He's shady as hell. Have you seen how he treats his mother?"

"Everyone is shady as hell in this town. I don't ask how you make your money," she calls me out. Savio and I hijacked a load of stereos and sold them to make money just last week.

"He's exactly like your father." My eyes stay pinned on her. Each muscle in my face hardens like stone as I think about the asshole.

"We all know history repeats itself around here," she whispers, moving her body away, but I pull her back in.

"I'm not trying to fight with you. I just worry. There are so many other guys," I say.

"None that are my age."

As I stare down at Demi, I can't stop thinking how beautiful and smart she is. She refuses to see it and I don't know how to *make* her. "Maybe you need to look at the ones a year older." I puff out my chest and she fucking chuckles. My lips purse harder as I take the slam to my ego.

She bumps me on the shoulder before replying, "If only you dated."

This is my moment. My mouth needs to open and say I would date her. I would do everything in my power to make her happy.

A slamming door draws our attention to her house. Her father gets into his car and speeds away. "He won't be back tonight. I'll be safe." She sighs. "I should go home and make sure my mom is alright." I hate the guilt that washes over her beautiful features. What she doesn't say is he was hellbent on hitting someone. If it's not her, it's her mom.

"Yeah, I understand. I'll keep the ladder up in case you need to use it in the middle of the night."

"Thank you, Dante." She leans in and surprises me by kissing my cheek and the edge of my lip. *Holy fucking hell.*

She moves to the ladder and I'd normally help her down, but most of my muscles have forgotten to work. My dick is the only one doing its job, hard as a rock, and I'm left giving her some shitty ass wave. I watch her limp across the road and sneak into her house.

"Tell Demi you love her yet?" Savio dips his head through my window.

"Go to Hell." He chuckles at my comeback. "Her father hit her again." That rage I felt returns as my lips flatten and my pulse roars to life. "I promised her he would never do it again."

I look my brother in the eyes, hoping he knows what I'm asking and he won't make me say it aloud. *Please beat the fucker to death.*

"He still at home?" Savio looks at their house, then back to me.

"I wouldn't have let her go back if he was."

"I have your back." We fist bump each other. "Don't forget to sleep with one eye open." It's a reminder that my mother will be coming for her pound of flesh as payment for leaving her family dinner. Savio slides out onto the roof and starts down the ladder.

"Where are you going?" I ask.

He gives me a smile and a wink. "Tonight will be the last time Demi's father hits her. Did you want to come?"

I look toward Demi's house. "I'll stay to make sure he doesn't return." I would love nothing more than to watch him take his last breath, but I can't leave Demi vulnerable to him returning.

"He won't. You have my word." Savio nods.

"Thanks, Savio."

"What else are brothers for?" He gives me a salute and hops down onto the grass.

Chapter 2

Demi

6 months later

My mother latches the strap of my right heel that's one size too small for me. I wish her feet would grow so that my toes weren't crushed every time I needed to borrow her shoes. She places my foot down onto a fast-food wrapper lying on the ground. It crunches under my heel, the sound louder than it should be.

Between school and my part-time job, I haven't had time to clean the house. My mother stays in her bed all day, allowing the bills to pile up and I'm left with all the responsibility on my shoulders. This is the first day she's gotten herself out of bed in six months.

"You're a good girl, Demi. Just remember, if you are nice to them, they will be nice back." I nod, my eyes going from my foot to the ugly red past due letter hanging on the door. I swallow down my nerves.

My mother continues in a low whisper, causing me to strain to hear her. "I would never ask this of you, but if we don't pay the bank by tomorrow, they'll evict us. I don't want you to be sleeping on the streets, honey."

My eyes glide to my mother as she does up my other shoe. "Your father used to bring home most of the money. With him gone…" Her words trail off and her eyes tear up. "I can't keep up."

His leaving was the best thing to happen to either of us in as long as I can remember. If she could just be well enough to get out of bed, she could help me and we could make this work.

"You need to get out of bed regularly, Mom. I ran into Annabeth and she said she could use your help at the daycare again. It would help with the bills piling up."

The tears glistening in her eyes begin to spill over her lashes. She wipes them away with her palm, giving me a tired look. "I am trying really hard, Demi." She grabs hold of my hand. "I promise I will be better. Tomorrow, I'll go see Annabeth."

I smile and squeeze her hand back. This is the fourth time she's promised this. I'm left hoping that one day it will sink in and she'll actually follow through.

I stand, wearing one of her old dresses. It's a little snug, exposing my cleavage, and its skirt will show my bottom the second I bend over or sit.

"Make me proud, Demi. I love you." She kisses my cheek—with the first smile on her face I've seen in six months—as she appraises me. I don't think she even realizes it's my birthday today. I know she doesn't. She wouldn't even be able to say what month it is if I asked.

"Will you be up when I get home?" I ask.

She shakes her head. "I'll be in bed. Come give me a kiss to let me know you made it back."

I walk out the door on shaky legs, my entire body trembling as my keys jingle together in my hand. Before getting into my family's car, I pause, glancing at the roof of the Mancini's, hoping to see Dante. If he saw me, I know he would fix this somehow. Still, I'm flooded with relief that he'll never know what my mother is making me do. I don't know if I could look him in the face if he knew. The world doesn't care that I'm poor. I need to toughen up or I'll be eaten alive in this town where there's always someone looking to scam their next victim.

I dig into my small clutch and pop a mint into my mouth hoping to calm my nervous stomach, before I turn the ignition to begin the journey to my first client. My hands quiver as I drive, shaking *almost* as fast as the heart beating against my ribs.

It's not like I'm a virgin.

Slowing down at the intersection that my mother directed me to, I spot the man she described standing there. I hand roll the window down and give him a pretty smile—just like my mother told me.

"John?" I ask, fighting back the urge to laugh at my own inside joke.

The man frowns. "I think names are best left out, sweetheart."

He walks to the passenger side door and looks around to double check no one he knows sees him. My stomach swooshes. It's a good thing we haven't had food in our house for two days now.

I look at his left hand to see if there is a ring on it. Nothing. *Thank goodness.* I drive back toward our side of town.

"I can see you got your prettiness from your mother." He places his hand on my leg. I have to fight to not squirm away. My face muscles hurt as I force my smile to stay on my face. I nod, not saying anything. The less I talk, the more they will like me.

This is a one-time deal. My mother said so herself. We just need this to make the bills.

I pull into a dark alleyway not too far from my house. I'm familiar with the location and it gives me a sense of security. If I scream for help, someone might recognize my voice and come to help if I need it.

I place the car in park, turning off its lights.

"Should we get into the back?" I ask, turning to the passenger seat. The man is already out of the car and opening the back door before the sentence leaves my mouth. *I guess so.*

I walk to the back and take a deep breath to calm my nerves before I pull on the handle. I sit in the dark backseat and see his semi hard cock already out. My stomach cramps and I force myself to lean in and try to kiss the guy.

"I don't kiss." The man moves back from me. "Your mother said you knew how to do this."

It's too dark to see my expression, otherwise he'd see my face paling as all the blood rushes from it. *This is actually going to happen.*

"Money first." I hold my hand out, remembering my mom said to always get payment upfront.

"Yes, yes, of course." He lifts his ass off the seat and pulls his wallet out.

He hands me a wad of cash. I flip through it. "This is all ones."

"It's all there. You don't get a tip until the end, *if* I end up enjoying it." I lift a brow and force my teeth to bite my tongue.

I take my time to count each dollar bill. For two hundred bucks, you would think the stack would be thicker. I can't believe I'm doing this for a measly two hundred. He lunges at me and his hands paw at my chest.

"Wrap that dirty mouth around my cock," he demands, and I freeze. *I can't.* Sleeping on the street can't be that bad, can it?

The back door opens and the man flies backwards from the car, screaming like a little girl. The sound of fists hitting flesh carries through the shadows in a steady, never ending song of deliverance. It's a sound I recognize well because of my father, but tonight it carries a different tenor. I step out of the car, ready to stop the assault. My mother is going to blame this mess on me, without a doubt.

"Stop!" I yell, gripping the assaulter's thick forearm. Both of my hands cling to him as I desperately beg him to stop.

"What the fuck, Demi?" I freeze at the sound of Dante's voice over the other man's moaning from the ground. "Get the fuck away from her. If you ever come near her again, I will murder you."

"She owes me two hundred bucks!" he spits.

"Like fuck she does. I'm giving you ten seconds to get out of my face before I drop you off on your wife's doorstep."

He considers pressing the issue for a moment, then scrambles to get up and limps away into the night.

Dante's facial features are hard, his lips curled into a snarl as he pins me with a stare. My cheeks flush and shame washes over me before the reality of what just happened slams into my chest. I can't have my mother hearing about this. We desperately need the money. The two hundred bucks is the partial interest we owe. More bills will come in next week and she'll send me out again, a neverending cycle of trying to make ends meet.

"You can't get involved with this, Dante! It's none of your business!" I yell. "Without that money, my mother and I are going to be homeless."

"Selling your body for sex is *not* the fucking answer!" Dante bellows in argument.

"I have no other option!" My hands fly up in the air as I defend my decision no matter how embarrassed I am. "That two-hundred dollars is keeping a roof over my head." I look back into the car, gesturing to all the one dollar bills scattered around the back seat.

"Two hundred bucks, Dem?" His voice breaks and embarrassment flares hot in my chest once again. "If you're going to take money to fuck someone, then fuck me." He presses his hard body into mine. He towers over me and I have to crane my neck to keep looking at him. I try to stand tall without shrinking back into myself.

His lips catch me off guard when they crash into mine. The kiss is hard and possessive, even though it only lasts a quick second. I stumble backward from the sudden jolt of our bodies being pushed together. My hands grip his forearms to keep me upright and there's a hunger to his demeanor as his hands slip down my sides and lift me by the back of my thighs. The cool metal hood he places me on has me gasping at the contrast of temperature; my body is overheating, feeling more alive than it ever has.

He descends on me like a vulture, his lips trailing a scorching trail down my neck as he nudges his hips between my legs and I pant for air. His masculine pine scent cloaks me, fills me, and the warmth I associate with his smell spreads through me.

He has always been the one person I can depend on in this world. This should feel wrong, but those thoughts never come. I don't care the reason he's kissing me, when he kisses me like he owns me. I want to live in this moment and not let the reality of our ugly world ruin it for me.

My legs lock behind his ass, bringing him in closer. His lips move down to my chest. My partially torn top allows him to easily move my breast from behind the fabric. He takes my nipple into his mouth, his warm tongue circling the super-heated flesh before he flicks at its peak. He cups my other breast, squeezing it lightly, as I moan at the sensation of him sucking my nipple. His touches are making me believe in Heaven.

His other hand slides down my body and draws small circles on my exposed inner thigh. His fingers press up then slide back down, teasing. "Did he rip the panties off you or did you come like this?" he asks as he switches breasts.

I don't want to answer.

His fingers part my labia, running over my clit before they enter me. A low growl erupts when he finds me soaking wet. All for him. "Damn it, Dem! Tell me if this is for him or me."

"It's always been for you," I angrily spit. "Fuck you for even asking."

He pulls away, studying my face. I'm unable to look past his gaze, captivated by the raw emotions behind his eyes.

"What if someone sees us?" I ask, looking around the dark alleyway.

"Then, I'll fucking kill them." I gulp at the ferocity in his words.

His fingers work at the button of his pants but he never looks away. "Feel it. This is what you do to me." I reach for his cock. My fingers wrap around it and I feel it grow under my touch. My hand strokes his length. It's smooth and hard, thick veins warm in my grip.

He removes his hand and enters me with one quick thrust. I moan, welcoming the way he stretches me, and my vision blurs momentarily as my breath leaves me in a whoosh. He moves in and out at a slow, leisurely pace. I circle my hands around his neck to hold on, hiding my face in the space between his shoulder and face, never being more ashamed of myself. Tears prickle at my eyes, no matter how many times I try to blink them away. I'm being fucked out in the open on the hood of a car like a prostitute.

"Fuck, you feel amazing," he moans.

I move his face to kiss my lips. My insides flutter for him when he kisses me back and I try to convince myself it's not like that with him. He sees me as more than just a fuck. With each thrust, I soar higher, losing myself in the way he plays with my body. His one hand tweaks my nipple and I'm a goner. I moan out his name, unable to stay quiet.

Dante growls, "Fuck, Demi!" His hips swirl and he shoves himself impossibly deep inside of me as he releases himself. We're both left panting into the crooks of each other's necks.

Placing a soft kiss on my cheek, he slowly pulls out. I watch in fascination as a small drop of cum drips onto my car before he tucks himself back into his pants.

"Here's two hundred bucks." He slaps the money into my hand and I flinch like I've been slapped. My eyes are wide; my heart has no time to slow. I jump off the hood of the car, straightening my destroyed dress.

"Fuck you! I'm not taking your money, Dante."

He gets right into my face. "The fuck you're not. If your mother forces you to whore yourself out, it might as well be to me." My stomach drops and I think I'm going to be sick. I didn't fuck him for the money.

Anger washes over his hard features and he suddenly looks so much older than nineteen. "This is my life, Dante. None of us can avoid the road we're set upon. You think I *wanted* to do this tonight? To sell my body for money? It sickened me. I thought maybe out of everyone, maybe you would understand since you know me so well."

He snorts his stupid response, refusing to say anything. It makes me even angrier.

"What the hell were you doing out here tonight, anyway?" I ask.

He digs into his front pocket and places a small gold bracelet into my palm. "Happy fucking birthday." He turns on his heels, leaving me standing by my car with his cum dripping down my leg.

I hold up a beautiful, thin gold bracelet with a small key pendant. He remembered it was my birthday. The last time I got any type of gift, I think I was seven, and it was a stuffed animal from my mother. With blurry vision, I look at the bracelet once again. It's the most beautiful gift I've ever seen. I clutch the delicate chain in my palm and hold it to my aching chest.

I refuse to make a sound when tears start to pour over my lashes and down my cheeks. I weep for the life I was never privileged enough to have, and for always wanting more. The hope of a better future seems like an ugly joke which continues to dangle in front of me, yet is always just out of my grasp.

Dante walks away with powerful strides, his sculpted back rippling beneath his t-shirt. I hold my breath, hoping for him to change his mind and come back to apologize. It's that hope I cling to, but when he lets me down, well, that squeezes my heart. He never once looks back.

I turn toward my rusted car, forced to step over a used needle to get to the driver's door. In this world, I'm the only person who can make my life better. The fairytale of Dante is exactly that, a foolish dream I can't afford to have.

I vow to myself that I'll graduate with honors and make a life I love that's far from the drain of this side of the tracks. I'm done with suffocating in this town. I'm going to make something of myself, and hold my head up; proud of the life I'll build for myself. When people remind me what I had to endure, I'll look them in the eyes and tell them I survived then ask how their life is going in the same town with the same people, while I was lucky enough to have escaped.

I can't get hurt if I refuse to give people that kind of power over me. I'm going to get out of this town one day, and I'm going to show everyone that there's more to me than they all think.

Chapter 3

Dante

Present day

I walk into my strip club and find two of the girls dancing on center stage in the middle of the room.

"Hey, boss man," Sienna, my head bartender, greets me. She's the only woman in this room I don't own.

"I heard Savio is having a huge birthday bash for his wife. Think you can get me an invite?"

I lift a brow. "Why would you want to go?"

She wipes down the counter in front of her. "I'm all about who you know, not what you know. That party is going to be filled with contacts that could be useful in the future."

I place my hands in my pockets. "Sure. I'll place you down as my plus one."

"Perfect!" She comes around the counter and places a kiss on my cheek. My body tenses at the contact. "So, there's been some girl coming around here looking for a job."

I take a seat on the stool and she moves back behind the bar to pour a glass of water for me. "She owe us a debt?" I ask, confused.

Anyone who knows my reputation stays far away from this place and me. The only women who come to me for work are in *some* kind of trouble, the kind of trouble that doesn't accept a payment plan. When I hire them, I pay their debts on day one, no questions asked. In return, I own them, which means I protect them as long as they show up to work and stay out of trouble, until every cent is paid back. That's how I've gotten all of my staff, except Sienna.

"Nope. Never heard of the girl. Her name isn't in our ledger. I asked around, but she's a nobody. Looks clean too."

I take a sip of the water. "Then why the hell would she want to work here?" I know the rumors of this place. Everyone knows once you start here, you never leave. I will own you for life.

"I tried to talk her out of it," she says with a shrug. "Twice. If the girl is stupid enough to come a third time, I think we should give her a shot."

I nod in agreement. "Same as always. You conduct the interview and I'll watch."

Sienna looks at her phone. "She'll be here in half an hour."

I stand, waving her off as I head into my office.

I have Sienna conduct all the interviews. If a girl can't give a dance to another woman, she's too weak to work here. And this way, I've also ensured that there's no man taking advantage of them. I'm not as ruthless as everyone says. Every one of my girls has a better life working for me than they could if they had been allowed to continue on their own paths.

I move my computer mouse around and begin my work. I'm going to have to send Savio after two guys tomorrow who are late paying.

The light on my wall flashes, indicating the audition room is in use. I pour myself a drink and go toward the two-way mirror. The new girl's back is to me. She's wearing a short, high waisted black skirt and a crop top. Her hair is long and cascades down her back in soft waves. Her nails are painted black and short.

Sienna keeps talking to her and sits in the chair, ready for her lap dance. The brunette walks over to the tablet and looks like she's picking a song. She sways her ass with a nice rhythm, gracefully swiveling her hips over Sienna's lap. I wonder if this girl has had real dancing lessons. Maybe this is her rebellious stage as a *fuck you* to her rich parents.

When she turns, my heart stops. My glass slips through my fingers and my past is looking me dead in the eye. It's like she knows I'm watching through the mirror. Her eyes stay locked on mine as she dances and gives me a sly, sexy grin.

This is the first and only girl I ever said I love you to, and then she vanished. I was the one who helped her out of every one of her bad decisions, and the only thanks I ever got was a giant *fuck you* when she disappeared without a word. If she had ever loved me, she would have chosen me instead of the road.

My feet move of their own accord and I fling the door open, its handle hitting the wall. Demi stills and Sienna stands, moving Demi out of the way. I've never interrupted Sienna before. Her eyes are wide with worry, unsure of what to do.

"I'll take it from here, Sienna."

She knows better than to argue with me. She nods and slips out, closing the door after her.

"What the hell are you doing here, Demi?"

Demi mirrors my shocked expression. Staring into her gorgeous emerald eyes, our past slams into me. I wish I could hold on to the good times in this moment, but they seem to have been too few and far between.

"I could ask you the same thing!" Defiance blazes in her eyes. Her right lip curls as she looks down her nose at me, like I'm some skeezy douchebag patronizing a strip club.

"I own this club and everyone in it. You want to become mine? Because last time you had the chance, you ran away."

"I thought the mafia owned this place?"

"I *am* the mafia, darling." I can't keep the condescending tone from my voice.

"From stereo heists to mafia boss, huh? Here I thought we'd be left in that horrible town for the rest of our lives. Look at us, out of that hellhole."

"*I'm* out of that hellhole. *You* just managed to find a new one. Just like old times, I see. Now, tell me why the hell you're here."

I hardly survived when she walked out on me all those years ago. I'd had a plan, a ring, and I was getting us the hell out of there. Now she's here and just as beautiful as she'd been back then and I'm not sure I'm man enough to survive her again.

"I need a job." She huffs, crossing her arms across her chest.

"The diner is hiring. It's in my territory. You can start tomorrow." My tongue runs across my teeth.

"I can't survive on pancake and coffee tips." Demi steps closer and her hand rests on my forearm.

I grip her arm, turning it roughly in my grip as I inspect her. No track marks to be seen. Her eyes look clear and alert. *Sober.*

"What's the drug of choice?" I ask.

"Excuse me?" She takes a step back, insulted.

"If you need money bad enough to work here, my extensive experience tells me that you have a problem. So I'll ask one more time, what's the drug of choice? Heroin? Coke? Fentanyl is much cheaper, but it'll kill ya' in a couple of years."

"You know me better than that. I don't do drugs."

"You *used* to not do drugs. I don't know you anymore," I correct.

"What happened to the boy next door?"

I give her a cruel smile. "He grew up."

Demi

I ignore his intimidating stance. "Please, Dante," I beg, dragging him to the chair before pushing him down into it. My music continues to play in the background and I try to get back into the right head space. The room is smaller than it felt before and my heart is beating like crazy. Keeping my head up high, I force my pride to stay intact and swivel my hips, trying to show him I can dance, that I'll make him proud.

He stands up and grabs my wrists, his fingers biting into my skin. "I'm not interested in something I've already had," he seethes.

I should have expected Dante's harsh words. His eyes have hardened over the years, making him no longer resemble the boy I once knew. I hate knowing that I had anything to do with the transition from the boy I grew up with to the man standing before me. He doesn't have to tell me he thinks I ghosted him by never returning. It was never that simple. Our connection never was.

But he'd told me he loved me and I left him anyway.

My mind is forced back to our past when my mother would send me out once a week to sell my body. Each week I came back with the two hundred bucks Dante gave me. Every time I came over, I saw it killed him a little more. It strained our friendship and I never felt like I deserved more.

"I need this job. I've never asked you for anything before." Tears glisten in my eyes. If my mother could see me right now, she would call me pathetic. I'm weak and desperate. "Do it for the girl who lived next door."

A sarcastic laugh rips from his throat. "You stopped being that girl on your eighteenth birthday. That's the day you stopped being my friend and I became the guy who dug you out of holes." He shakes his head, releasing my wrists. "You never had to ask me for anything because I loved you so much; I did it before you had to ask."

Tears leak over my dark lashes, making him appear blurry. "I'm a hard worker."

"Every time you snuck into my bedroom for sex, did I make you feel like a whore?" His voice starts soft and grows louder. A sob breaks free of me. "Answer me Demi!"

I shake my head, trying to gain my voice back. "No. You never made me ask, and I'd always find the money in my pocket once I got home."

"What did I promise you when your father hit you for the last time?"

I can't stop my crying. I have blocked out so much of this, thinking it was better to forget than to live with the memories. I shrug my shoulders, still crying.

"You don't even fucking remember." He scoffs. "How much money do you need to make?"

Dante is pacing back and forth in front of me. His eyes no longer light when they see me. Instead, they look mean.

"I need four thousand a month." I hiccup.

"What type of interest are you paying? I'm better off buying you, and then you can work it off for me." He stops pacing and turns to me. "Give me the name and I'll fix this."

The thing is, he can't fix this problem and I can't bear any more disappointing looks from him.

"Do I have the job? It's a yes or no, Dante." I'm finally able to stifle my tears. "Like you said, you can't be saving me from every problem I land myself in."

"Four thousand? No dancer of mine makes that by just dancing." For the first time, his eyes soften and pity makes its way into his stare. I hate it.

"Yes or no, Dante?" I hold my ground, trying to stiffen my legs as they tremble. If I stand here much longer, I'm going to fall to the ground and curl up to cry my troubles away.

"I can't get you four thousand, and you'll sell your pussy over my dead fucking body. I didn't do what I did back then for you to run right back to it." He points his finger at me.

"Can you give me a job? That's all I'm asking. I'll figure out the money thing after."

He runs a hand through his hair, his muscular biceps stretching the fabric of his collared shirt.

"Clean up your face and then go see Sienna at the bar. It will be up to her. She's the one who does the hiring." He walks out, slamming the door behind him.

I breathe in through my nose and out through my mouth, trying to calm myself down. Nothing is helping. If I open my mouth to speak, I'll end up crying all over again. There's no way Sienna will hire me if I'm on the verge of a panic attack.

I leave the room, not even glancing at the bar, and rush out of the building.

Chapter 4

Dante

"D<small>EMI</small> G<small>ALLO</small>," I <small>MUTTER</small> her name and place my head in my hands. My elbows rest on the hard surface of my desk. I had convinced myself I would never see her again.

I'm fine.

I stand, wanting to go straight to Sienna to ask when she starts, but resist the urge. *Fuck!* Seeing Demi has sent me back ten years as if it were yesterday.

"*What's with the ring?*" Savio asks, stepping into my bedroom.

I meet his eyes in the mirror. I've been standing here looking between the cross burned into my chest and the ring. Our mother had caught me asleep and took the opportunity to deliver my punishment.

"*If I'm going to get Demi to leave with me, she needs some sort of promise.*"

"I didn't realize you two were dating." He eyes me cautiously.

I turn to look at him, shoving the ring into my pocket. "We haven't labeled what we are."

He's still staring at me and I feel obligated to explain. "Look, I realize our relationship isn't normal or conventional, but we get each other. We both feel it."

"You sure? Because I just saw her making out with her boyfriend."

My heart twists. "She's going to come with us. If you have a problem with it, tell me now."

He raises a hand in surrender. "No problem. I must have seen wrong."

He leaves my room, closing the door behind him. My body itches to storm over to her house and demand to know what's going on. Instead, I force myself to lie down on my bed. My hands rest above my head, holding on to the headboard to keep me in place.

From this position, I can stare out my window. The evening sky has gone from red to black within an hour.

"Dante?" Demi pokes her head into my room. I wait for her to announce why she's here, continuing my vacant watch of the night in silence. She crawls through the window and lies down on the bed with me. Her breathing quickly matches mine, no words spoken for long minutes, and it's almost easy to pretend like there's nothing wrong.

"How's Jameson?" I lift my head to watch her reaction.

She sighs. "He's not you."

"That's right. You only show up when you want my cock."

"Well, it is a beautiful cock." She kisses my jaw. "But that's not why I'm here tonight." Her kisses trail over my cheek to my lips.

I grip her hips and lift her to straddle me. "What if I told you I love you and I don't want to share you with anyone? Ever." My heart rate doubles. I'm not the type of guy who puts himself out there to be rejected. I've experienced enough of that in my lifetime, I don't need more memories.

"Do you love me?" Her smile is dazzling and bright right now.

"I do love you." I swallow around the lump in my throat.

"You are the sweetest man I have ever met."

Not exactly the reaction I was going for.

Her hand moves my jaw back to look at her. "I love you too. I wish I could pay you back for everything you have ever done for me."

"It's never been like that for us. Run away with me, Demi. We've talked about getting away from here. I have a plan. We can have that life we talked about." The ring is burning a hole in my pocket, but I decide to wait and slip it on her finger the moment we're out of here. It will be the first page of our new chapter.

"When do we leave?" She laughs, not understanding that I'm serious.

I flip her under me. My arms rest on either side of her head. "I'm serious. Once Savio ties up a few loose ends, we're gone."

Her fingers lightly trace my scabbed-up burn. "Is it because of this?"

"No, it's because you deserve more and I want to be the man who makes that a reality. I want to watch your face light up. I want to be the one you allow to love you."

"Kiss me like you love me," she pleads.

I take a shot of whiskey, remembering how she used me make me feel invincible, like I was her everything. When she was around I used to want to be a better person. I was naive enough to think all we needed was love. I scoff. There's no such thing as love in the life I live.

I steeple my fingers above the bridge of my nose, trying to forget all memories of Demi. My fingers fan out to rub my eyes, then temples.

A knock at my office door has me calling, "Come in."

My stomach flutters, hoping to hear more information about Demi. My traitorous cock perks up just at the thought of her. The door opens, and it's not Sienna as I had expected, but one of my older brothers, Maximus. Disappointment joins the party, worsening my already bad mood.

Max is the second oldest out of us four boys still alive. He's a bit of a recluse and lives in the woods, rarely—as in never—comes out for social visits.

"Nice joint you have going here," he says upon entering.

I push myself to stand and shake his hand. "Thank you. What are you doing in town?" My forced smile hurts, feeling like fish hooks are holding it up in place.

"Savio guilt tripped me about never meeting his new wife. He said since I missed the wedding, I can't miss her birthday party."

"You need a date? I can have that arranged." It's so much easier to talk business. I'm able to push the thought of Demi out while I consider who might go well with Maximus.

He laughs. "I can find my own dates, thank you. But I'll take a drink if you have one."

I loosen the tie around my neck, its silky length choking me. "That, I can do!" I walk to the side of the room that hosts my mini bar and pour us both a drink from my flask. Her face reappears in my mind but I refuse to allow her to take up space. I take a quick swig of whiskey before pouring the same amount for both of us. We clink our glasses together and I down the amber liquid, welcoming its harshness.

I haven't thought about Demi in nine years. I honestly never thought I'd ever see her again.

Now that I have, I'm not sure I ever want to again.

I tilt my head back, opening my mouth, and wait for the flow of whiskey to enter my mouth. Nothing. My feet stumble back two steps as I bring the flask opening to my eye. One lousy drop hangs on to the metal, begging to fall into my mouth. My tongue darts out, stealing the last drop before I toss the useless container into my brother's perfectly manicured hedge.

The front door falls open with a slight push and it has me tripping over my feet as I make my grand entrance. I squint, trying to merge all the different bodies into one image. By the amount of people, I'd say every Italian on the eastern seaboard was invited. It's obvious my brother spared no expense for his wife's birthday. He's a fool, allowing himself to be guided by his heart. Love is going to get him killed sooner or later. He's just shown his hand and now everyone knows Charlotte is his ultimate weakness.

My legs cross in front of each other as I attempt to walk straight. I don't think I've ever been this out of sorts. I'm the calm one. The collected one. The one whose control is on a short leash tightly gripped in my steady hand.

Usually.

"You okay, boss?" Sienna walks up to me with concern washing over her face.

"I'm fine." She attempts to straighten my tie and I pull it loose once again. "When does Demi start?" I ask, brushing her hands away from me.

"Who?"

I scratch at my head. Did I imagine Demi? "The girl you interviewed." My voice wavers as I think I've lost my mind.

"Remember, you took over the interview." She gives me a pointed look.

"Yes, but I told her to ask you if she got the job. Didn't she stop by the bar after?"

"I watched her walk out of the club. She didn't even look twice at the bar." She places a hand on my shoulders. "Are you okay, Boss?"

I forcefully remove her hand. "You know I don't like being touched."

"You're getting better at it though."

Sienna's concern annoys me. Demi blowing off the chance for a job she begged for infuriates me. Demi should have asked Sienna when she started. Why the hell didn't she?

"You sure you're okay?"

I wave her off.

I don't know why seeing Demi hit me so hard. She didn't even want the job. I'll probably go another ten years or longer before I ever see her again. I laugh at how silly I'm being. Sienna gives me a look like I've gone crazy, but walks away silently.

It's fine.

I'm fine.

Everything is fine.

I walk further into the house and find Savio dancing with his wife, Charlotte, on the dance floor. Everyone's eyes are on the new couple. I never thought my brother would fall in love, but here he is.

The fool.

Chapter 5

Demi

It's official, I've hit rock bottom. Digging into my pocket, I have two bills and some change. It's enough money for a motel room and just enough gas to go see my mother. I shudder, thinking about how *that* conversation will go.

My eyes glance up at the strip club's blinking neon sign: Throne of Sin. My shoulders sag in defeat as the realization hits that there's only one option left now. I pull at the car door handle three times before it unsticks and opens.

"You okay, Mom?" My nine-year-old daughter, Oakleigh, asks between coughs. I rub her back until the fit has left her. I knew sleeping on the cold floor would spark a flareup in her lung disease and cause pneumonia. Even though the doctors assured me that her bronchopulmonary dysplasia at birth was nothing related to my pregnancy, I still go through and analyze everything I think I could have done better. Luckily she was able to outgrow it but her lungs are still weak. Between her asthma and her chronic pneumonia, it seems like she's always coughing and on the verge of being sick.

"Everything is great," I lie. "Have I ever told you about your grandmother?"

Oakleigh's eyes light up. "No, why?"

"You, my girl, will get to meet her today." I lean in and give her a kiss on the cheek.

Her hands run through her hair in an effort to tame her long locks. Twisting the key into the ignition is harder than I thought it would be when I know where I'm going, and who I'm hoping to leave my daughter with. I promised myself I would never allow my mother near Oakleigh, but I have no choice.

We pull into the neighborhood I grew up in, the car running on fumes, and lurch onto the cracked driveway of my childhood home. Even with the car stopped, my hands grip the wheel. If I let go, my daughter will see how badly I'm shaking.

My tongue darts out to lick my lips. "Here goes..." I blow out a deep breath. "Come on, Oakleigh." We both open our doors and stare out at the house that could use a new paint job. We stand there, side by side, for several long seconds before she takes my hand and looks up at me, an eyebrow arched in question.

"Want a candy?" My daughter hands me a small red hard candy. I smile, taking it from her and placing it in my mouth, sucking on the sweet flavor.

There's a big sign taped to the broken siding informing visitors that the doorbell is broken. I knock three times as loud as my hand can pound.

"Go away!" a grumpy voice yells from inside. "I'm not interested in buying anything."

We both look at each other. We could sleep in the car for a few nights...

Oakleigh begins to cough over and over, unable to catch her breath. She brings out her inhaler and takes a deep breath of the last of her medicine, but it doesn't even sound like anything came out. I bang my hand on the door for a second time.

My mother opens the door with a scowl on her face. Seeing me her eyes soften and shock radiates through her for a moment before she composes herself and her face turns back into a scowl. She quickly covers it by asking, "What do you want?"

Oakleigh takes a step behind me and I hate my mother for not being the loving sort. I glance into the house and see my old cat, Stitches, try to slink her way outside. She still looks like a stray with parts of her coat missing.

My old cat walks outside and her tail curls around my leg. "Oakleigh, take Stitches out in the yard and play with her for a second." She does so with no questions or fuss, always well-behaved.

When she's out of earshot, I turn to my mother. "That is your granddaughter, not that you care."

Her lips twist, her only clear emotion being annoyance that I'm disturbing her day.

"Jameson came by a week ago looking for you. I told him this would be the last place you would ever come. But look at you here now."

I ignore her comment and get to the point. "I have to go away for a short while and I need you to watch Oakleigh for me." Both my mother's brows rise into her hairline. *I can't even believe I'm doing this.*

"You always were trouble. What type of mess did you get yourself into this time?"

"I'm not in trouble. It's just that Oakleigh has very expensive medication."

My mother cuts me off. "I can hardly feed myself and you want me to raise your child, feed her, *and* pay for medication?"

Frustration pricks at my nerves. I raise my hand in her face to stop her from saying anything else. "No, Mother. I will pay for all of that. For me to do that, I need to go out of town to work for a bit." At least, I hope it's for a little bit and not forever. I can't even fathom never seeing Oakleigh's beautiful face again. She's the reason I get up in the morning.

"I have no groceries. If I'm feeding her dinner, you will need to give me a hundred right away."

I dig into my pocket and pull out a few crumpled bills. "Here's twenty-five. It's all I have on me right now." I place it into my mother's wrinkled hand. "By tonight you'll receive a package of money, I promise. You need to buy her medication first, then the rest is yours for food and bills." Her eyes light up at the promise of money. I pull out a folded-up piece of paper that has my daughter's prescription scribbled on it in that penmanship that only doctors and pharmacists can read. "If you do one thing right for me, Mom, please take care of my little girl. Place her before yourself. She's the sweetest little girl you will ever meet. She's smart and caring. I promise she will listen and help you around the house." I clear my voice, trying to stay calm and unemotional.

"Fine," she concedes. Relief floods my nerves and I wrap my mother's fragile body in a hug.

"Thank you so much, Mom. This means the world to me." It's not that my mother was horrible or mean...she just never had the capacity to be there for me. I release my hold on her as she wiggles to get out of my grasp.

"What if Jameson comes by again?" she asks.

"You never saw me and hide Oakleigh." My heart rate rockets hearing Jameson's name and knowing I can't be here to protect my baby girl. I silently promise that I'll come and get Oakleigh as soon as I can.

"Oak!" I call out and she comes back with my cat in her arms. Stitches has never let anyone hold her, not even me.

"You be good for your grandma." I turn to my mom. "Mom, this is Oakleigh."

"Well, come on in, girl. Standing out there will make your cold worse." Oakleigh is ushered into my old house and the door is slammed in my face without further ado.

My throat tightens and it's hard to breathe. *I have to do this.* I suck in a breath but it comes in shallow, almost too little oxygen to breathe properly, and I begin to panic. The front window curtain moves and Oakleigh is standing there giving me a wave. I wave back and force myself off the steps. I don't want her to see me freaking out.

My body feels like it weighs a hundred tons as I walk back to my car. My leg bounces on the gas as I pull out of the driveway and drive away from my daughter, making it hard to keep speed. I pull toward an alleyway, hoping to siphon some gas to make it back into the city.

I end up having to stop three times to steal gas from other cars, but I'm able to make it back to the city with the red needle on empty once again. My car stops just before the seedy alleyway.

I walk toward the underground parking, trying to remember the directions I once heard. The building looks vacant but I know better. It's ironic how Jameson's threats of bringing me here used to scare me, and now I'm walking up willingly. The hairs on my arms stand straight the closer I get. *This is my last chance to earn enough money for Oakleigh.*

As I get closer to the famous red door that played a recurring role in my nightmares, I see the two guards holding machine guns. The moment I'm in their view, their barrels are aimed at me. They escort me through some underground passages and into a small room. It's cold, humid, and I can hear the faint sound of water dripping.

"What the hell is this?" The harsh sound comes from a man entering the room. He glares at me, then his guards. Goosebumps flow over my skin, highlighting every hair follicle on my arms.

My heart jackhammers, and I clear my voice. "I'm placing myself on sale." My spine straightens as he looks me over with a predatory gaze and I hold my breath, waiting for a response. He's scary looking, with scar pits on his face. So this is the man Jameson had threatened to send me to multiple times over the years. He traffics black market organs and women. My dreams didn't do him justice. He's way more frightening in real life.

"What the hell do you think we do here?"

My voice better not let me down. "Jameson told me to come to you," I lie. "You have an auction tonight and I want to be part of it." Surprisingly, my voice is strong and fierce.

"You're a little ripe for the pickings here tonight."

I raise a brow and my heart goes into my throat. "What do you mean?"

"You're old. The girls on sale tonight are young, beautiful, and innocent. The men in that room like virgins. But you look healthy... let me take a kidney." He walks up and touches my stomach feeling what I'm assuming is my kidney. His hands are rough and I automatically step away from his touch. My stomach twists sharply. Looking around the room there's no escape now.

"You're forgetting men like experience. Put me on the stage." His eyes cast down my body with disgust, and disinterest. He nods to his guards and one of them pokes their gun into my back.

"Please." I fall to my knees. "I have to do this. The only thing I ask is for you to send my mother a thousand dollars every week for five months."

"Women don't return to their lives. This isn't some resort you book for your family vacation."

I'm crying, even though I'm trying like Hell not to. "I have no other choice," I beg. "Put me on first, before they see the others." I hold on to his legs. "All I ask is that you send my mother a thousand a week until you reach ten thousand." That will give me two or three months to get back to my daughter.

"I'm not a bank. What the hell was Jameson thinking sending you here? You're useless to me."

"Please. A thousand tonight and a thousand every week until you reach ten thousand," I negotiate.

He wiggles his foot with a disgusted curl on his lips, trying to get me to let go of his feet. "I'll send the money, but only if you get bought. If not, you get nothing and I get to take your kidney for free."

This is the worst decision of my life but there's no turning back now. "Thank you, thank you." I can't believe I'm thanking this man. I use both hands to wipe the tears from my face. My girl is finally going to get the medication she needs. She'll be able to be healthy and run and play like all children should.

"Get up from your knees and make yourself presentable. You're on in half an hour." I nod repeatedly. I will make this work.

I'm placed in a holding room with all the other girls. None of their eyes dare to travel up to meet mine. They are wearing white night gowns that remind me of the eighteen hundreds while I'm naked. Tex told me it's to remind the men that they like women with curves. I want to tell these girls to run back home and never return. It's all very hypocritical of me. I study each of their faces and promise myself that once I get my shit together, I will help these girls.

"You're on, Demi!"

Armed guards escort me through the cold narrow hallway and my nipples peak in the chilly air. I'm shoved through a curtain and onto a stage with lights that blind me.

The hand I'd been using to protect my modesty by at least *trying* to cover my breasts rises in an effort to keep the light out of my eyes.

"Spread them so we can see what we're buying," is called from below.

My stomach flips at the words and I cast my eyes down, deciding it's better just get it over with instead of trying to see beyond the stage lights. I pull in a deep breath, attempting to keep my knees from knocking together. My muscles are fighting against the freeze I've placed on them with the hopes of hiding how nervous I am. I want to turn around and say, "Not today, Satan..." but it's my way to save Oakleigh. She needs her medication more than she needs me. She deserves more than I ever had.

"The first girl of the evening," the announcer says from somewhere in the room.

The once rowdy room grows silent. My hands grip a lone stool in the middle of the stage. I can't bring myself to sit on it, but it helps to keep me steady as my hands hold on to it from behind me. Like the chair will save me.

More silence. I shift from foot to foot.

What if no one buys me? I want to be sick, the bright lights only making the feeling worse.

"Fifty thousand." My eyes snap up and I search for the bidder.

"Starting bid is one hundred thousand," the announcer reminds the room.

I swallow. They don't even want to pay the normal amount. My other realization is that Tex is making a pretty penny off my sale and has promised me almost nothing.

My chest tightens. There are beads of sweat that line my brow. This has to be a bad dream. I fight to stay upright as my head grows lighter and lighter.

"One hundred thousand." A man in the front row bids. He licks his lips and blows me a kiss. I take a step back, trying not to recoil. The stool wobbles, reminding me I have nowhere to go.

"One hundred and twenty-five thousand." The same man who offered fifty thousand bids. He sits in the back, a shadow cast over him except his shoes. He's wearing white sneakers, I think.

"One hundred fifty," an accented man calls out.

"Two hundred." The man in the front says, glaring at the competition.

My eyes have finally adjusted to the bright lights and I can now make out the hungry glint in the eyes of most of the men around me.

"Two fifty!" exclaims the heavy-set accented man with a double chin. His shirt has sweat stains around his belly.

Silence.

I look around, wishing there were better options here for me.

"Going once, going twice…" The announcer begins to close my bids up.

"Four hundred thousand," announces the sneaker man.

Shock radiates through the two men who were bidding for me.

"You can have her at that price." The one in the front row laughs, like I'm not worth that much. It pisses me off.

The thick accented man snickers. "He's the meanest one here, girl." The two men laugh at whatever inside joke they have going on.

Actually, the whole room chuckles. They're laughing at me.

The meanest one. My adrenaline spikes and I try to get a glimpse of the man who bought me.

"Sold!" The announcer officially sells me to the shadow man.

I stand tall for the first time tonight. I will not allow these men to laugh at me. There's a quick pinch to my neck, and my hand flies to the area. My head swivels to see a man walking away with a needle in his hand. My feet stumble as I try to stay standing. The lights are so bright they hurt my eyes.

Each muscle becomes heavy. My feet stumble again and I crash into the stool, we both go down and my vision goes black.

Chapter 6

Dante

"CHARLOTTE, CAN THIS WAIT?" I ask Savio's wife, who's just barged into my house like she owns it. She has the audacity to look refreshed while I'm still feeling the effects of my hangover. "Shouldn't you still be hungover from your birthday party?"

"It's been three days. My hangovers don't last days on end because I'm not old like you." I'd hardly call myself *old* at barely thirty, but I don't correct her.

She makes herself at home and pours a cup of coffee.

"Feel free to take my favorite mug as a to-go cup and leave." I try to wave her off but nope, she sits down and makes herself more comfortable.

My eyes glance toward the hallway then back at her. She immediately picks up on it. "What are you hiding back there?" She smiles over her steaming coffee.

"You said you had a reason to be here, right?" I cross my arms, pretending to be annoyed, but Charlotte has a way of making people like her and I'm far from immune to her charm. As a matter of fact, I find her rather amusing.

"Fine, fine. I think you could have a traitor at your club."

I grunt. Charlotte was held at gunpoint a while back and since then, she's adamant someone from the Italian mafia was in cahoots with her ex-best friend. She has been completely wrapped up with this conspiracy theory.

"Why are we beating a dead horse?" I ask, not understanding why this is still an issue. "Klaus is dead, why does this matter?" The problem is solved, end of story.

"Because it means we have an enemy in your club." She stands back up, jabbing me with her pointy finger. If she wasn't married to my brother, I would have broken the offending digit.

I glance back at the hallway. I really do have better things to do with my time today. A smirk forms on my lips as I remember what a great day it is.

"No, *you* have an enemy," I correct. I get her point, and I'll look into it, but I don't want her to think I'll just get up and do everything she wants. I'm not my brother.

"Dante!" she pleads.

I hold my hands up, placating. "I'll look into it. I promise."

"Where were you last night? You normally come over for dinner on Sundays." Charlotte and I have grown close since she got together with my brother, so I let her question slide, but her eyes keep sliding to the hallway every time I glance over there. She's way too nosey for her own good.

"You need to leave." I hold on to her arm and drag her a few steps toward the door.

"Why?" She smiles, enjoying herself way too much.

"I'm dealing with business. Last I checked, you had your own business that should take up your time."

A throat clears and both our heads swivel to the hallway. Demi is standing there in one of my old shirts I'd dressed her in while she slept. It doesn't even make it to her mid-thigh, and my mouth instantly dries at her image.

"Business, huh?" Charlotte mumbles under her breath with a chuckle. "I'll be going then, but I'm taking this mug with me."

Charlotte knows how to see herself out. I ignore her, my eyes locking on the woman I once knew as I walk toward her. "How are you feeling?"

She rubs her head and my shirt rises, giving me a glimpse of her shaven pussy before I avert my eyes back to hers.

"Why am I here?" Confusion riddles her tone and her eyes dart around the area.

"Because you're too stubborn to accept a job from me, but willingly sold yourself." I can't help the scoff leave my lips.

She nods. Her lips are pursed with uncertainty, like she still doesn't understand.

"I bought you," I confess, but I'm sure she's already come to the same conclusion.

"Wait!" Her hand goes to touch the spot where the needle pricked her. "What the hell was in that needle?"

"I have no control over that. That's how they do business. You're lucky that's the only thing that happened."

"Says the big mafia man who buys women."

"You're lucky it was me." I shake my head. "Look at you. Mad at me over something that's out of my control, when it's *your* stubborn ass that got you into that situation. Some things never change."

She crosses her arms over her chest glaring at me. *Fucking unbelievable.*

"I own everyone in my club. And that's where you will work until you pay off your debt. At that point, you will be welcome to leave or you can choose to stay. Up to you." I fight the urge to fiddle with my hands, needing them to be occupied; otherwise I'm liable to pull her in.

"That's going to take me like thirty years."

I rock my head back and forth. "Realistically, less than twenty. But with inflation, you never know. I don't charge interest. My first offer would have been better, but you're still as headstrong as you've always been."

I walk back to the kitchen area, giving myself space from her, and pour another cup of coffee, as well as one for her. "Coffee?" I place it on the counter, making her come to me.

She walks over, looking stunned and fragile. "Twenty years," she repeats in disbelief.

Maybe I should start charging interest... I don't know if I can let her walk out of my life again.

"I only have a few months. I can't stay longer than that." Her eyes are wide, flickering with worry. She's taking the news better than I imagined, and I realize she has no idea how bad it could have been.

"You don't have a choice. You're lucky it was me who bought you. Otherwise, you wouldn't have lived past the first year. I saved you." I spit with my words. She's so fucking clueless to the mess she willingly placed herself in.

"Once you're bought, you're bought for life. What the hell did you think was going to happen?"

She sets her hands around the warm mug but makes no effort to drink it. "I only have a year." She repeats as she slowly digests my words.

"When was the last time you ate?"

She looks up from her coffee. "Three days ago?"

Immediately, I pull out my frying pan and crack a few eggs into it. She just sits there, staring into her dark liquid. I don't have the heart to tell her that this lifestyle is easy for people like us. She has no family to speak of and lives in poverty. After a month working for me, she'll have family *and* money. All the girls protect each other, and they never go days without food. She'll never be hungry again. It might be too much at one time if I say this out loud, though. I'll let her get some food into her stomach and a hot shower before I introduce her to her new family.

Chapter 7

Demi

EVEN THOUGH I'M WALKING and talking, I feel like this is a dream. *This can't be my life.* I shake hands and smile at the other girls who also work for Dante. Dante's Girls, everyone calls them. The term family keeps getting thrown around and I want to scream and shout I already have a family. Instead, I keep everything locked in, buried deep, as I have to protect Oakleigh as much as I can.

Pressure sits heavily on my chest as Dante's bartender introduces me to an endless stream of women and I can't help but be dragged back into my past.

"Are you fucking Mancini?" Jameson bites my lower lip, his hands grip my hips with bruising pressure, keeping me between his legs. "You promised me you were my girl."

I pull away, tasting the metallic tang of blood. I've never been Jameson's girl. We had one date, to McDonalds, but he likes to keep tabs on me. He has that crazy look in his eyes. I should have listened to Dante and stayed far away from a guy like him.

He shakes me. "You're my girl, right?" His eyes slide from me to someone behind me.

"You okay, Demi?" I check over my shoulder to see Savio, Dante's brother. My cheeks flush pink with embarrassment. I came to talk to Jameson because my mother had an envelope for his mother, and this was the only way I could get it to her.

"She's just about to take my cock, of course she's okay. Unless you're here to watch like a perv?" Jameson responds for me.

I hit him in the chest and he laughs. No matter how hard I struggle, I can't get out of his grip. "Kiss me like you mean it, so Savio will leave," Jameson whispers into my ear. If I want to get away, I'm going to have to kiss him. I wrap my arms around him and press our lips together. It's my goodbye kiss. Soon, I'm never going to see this guy again. I can't believe I had a crush on him at one point.

Jameson is the one to pull away, and Savio is no longer in view. "You're a whore, just like your mother. How many men have you spread your legs for?" My hand comes up and slaps his cheek.

"Fuck you, Jameson."

He laughs in my face. "You'll be back before the end of the week, begging for my cum in you." He lets me go and I stumble from the sudden lack of force holding me to him.

I can't do this anymore. I don't know why I ever thought Jameson was someone I wanted to be around. I should have seen through all of his false compliments. Every time he hears I've been with Dante, he makes himself oppressively present. It's creepy how suddenly he appears.

I hug my purse under my arms, scared that the pregnancy test in there is going to grow legs and jump out of the bag. The walk home allows for my mind to run a hundred different directions, none of them going any place good.

The ladder that Dante keeps up is taunting me as I stare at it. I've never deserved someone like him in my life. He's the one I want to share the news of this pregnancy with. Once I tell him, he will make it better, but that creeping doubt overshadows anything positive.

My head peeks over the edge of the roof and Dante is sitting there with a smoke dangling out of his mouth. I've only seen him smoke one other time. His facial features are strained as his head tilts to the sky. I climb over and sit beside him. Immediately, he drags his arm around my shoulders. This is my safe place. It's the only place I truly ever want to be.

"We're getting out of this town." He blows the smoke up into the air and the wind has it scattering thin.

"That's always been the plan," I respond.

"Leave with me." He digs into his pocket and shows me the most beautiful ring I've ever seen. My mouth hangs open seeing it. "I'm done sharing. I want to start something amazing with you."

I can't answer. My mouth dries. That pregnancy test feels like it's pulsing its way from my purse into my heart.

"You don't mean that."

Dante uses his fingers to move my jaw, so we're staring into each other's eyes. "I do. I want to take care of you."

"I need to learn to love myself before I know how to do that with anyone else." All I can think about is the baby that's growing in my stomach. It's time I take responsibility. I can't be relying on Dante for everything.

"Do you love him?" I know he's referring to Jameson.

"No." The answer is quick and true. I never did.

He slips the ring on my finger. "I love you, Demi Gallo."

"Please, don't say that."

"I'm not expecting you to say it back." He sighs and removes his arm from around my shoulders. He leans back onto his elbows, his legs stretched out.

I stare at the ring. It would be the most unfair thing I've ever roped Dante into. My fingers tremble as I slip the ring off and place it back into his pocket.

"It's not the right time." I wish it was.

"Savio and I are leaving in the morning. Come with us."

The wings of hope flutter in my stomach. Can it really be that simple?

"Meet me back here, and that will be your answer. If you don't show, well, then I'll know."

My hand cups his jaw. "I have a few things I need to do first."

"You'll come?" Excitement flares over his face and he searches mine to see if I'm telling the truth.

"Yes!"

He kisses me, hard, like he doesn't believe me and this is our last kiss.

I didn't know he'd be right.

I never made it back to him, even though I tried.

Chapter 8

Demi

Present day

WELCOME TO THE THRONE *of Sin*. The large Throne of Sin sign illuminates the parking lot on my way in and a pit of dread settles in my stomach. Dante talks about family with these girls, but none of them like me. I can spot jealousy a mile away. I'll never gain their trust or friendship with Dante always at my back. Stepping inside, everyone ignores me as I make my way to the staff changing rooms and Dante goes to his office. Neither of us exchange words.

This is a means to an end. Friends would be a distraction from my goal. I slip on my black corset, its ribbon ties exposing most of my back while holding the girls up like they're on their own throne. I slip on the booty shorts that expose most of my fleshy white ass.

Two hours later, my arm aches from carrying around the black circular tray. A man from the VIP booth keeps catching my eye from every spot in the room. It feels like it's a game to him and each time I get that sensation of eyes on me, he smirks, catching my gaze.

"It took me months to catch TJ's eye." Robin pretends to pout as we place our trays down for more drinks. My hip leans against the bar as I look over my shoulder at the man she's talking about. Yup, he's still staring. "He's a big tipper. If he likes you, you can see your monthly income quadrupling just from him."

Dante's club is far from anything fancy, even though most of the clientele wear suits or suit jackets, but none of them look new or custom. There's a hardness etched in the way everyone holds themselves, like they are out for their pound of flesh. If I hadn't grown up the way I did, it would be intimidating.

"Stop gossiping." Sienna glares at Robin before taking my pad of paper and making my drinks.

Robin leans into my ear and says, "Sienna's just upset she's only allowed to bartend." I refuse to comment, not needing to make more enemies while I'm here.

With fresh drinks covering my tray, I lift it up and make my way back to the table. I place the round in front of each businessman at TJ's table.

"Anything else I can get you, gentlemen?" I ask.

TJ grabs my wrist and pulls me down onto his lap. I quickly glance around, not sure if this is okay, because it feels wrong. My heart rate increases and I try to stand back up.

"How is a girl as sweet as you in a joint like this?" he asks.

The way he's leering at me with his hand on my naked flesh makes me uncomfortable. So far, Dante has allowed me to serve, but nothing else. He keeps saying I'm not trained enough. Maybe this is normal, and I have to be okay with it. I try to calm my heart beat, because I need this job and I can't let Dante down.

TJ slips his arm around me, pulling me to the center of his lap. His erection grows harder and longer the more I squirm.

"Trust me, there's nothing sweet about me." I force a sweetness into my voice and flash him a strained smile. My eyes do a quick search of the room and not a single person looks concerned. In fact, I get a few glares from the other girls when they see whose lap I'm on.

His hot breath brushes over my neck. "That's what I'm hoping for."

I try to stand again just as TJ's once-tight grip loosens and I lose my balance. My hands fly in front of me to catch my fall, but they never hit the ground. Dante's possessive grip has me flush against his strong chest. Instantly, I breathe easier.

Inhaling his masculine scent, he easily maneuvers me behind him with his strong muscular back to me. I jump when a soft, warm hand takes mine before I see it belongs to Sienna.

"The drinks aren't going to serve themselves," she says, leading me away.

"No one gave me any new orders," I mumble as she continues to pull me toward the bar. I look over my shoulder, my feet stopping when I see Dante toss this TJ guy out of the club. The chatter around the room has stopped with all eyes following Dante. The large metal door slams with finality, its sound bringing everyone's gazes landing on me.

I cast my eyes to the ground, scolding myself for fucking up. Sienna leads me out of the main room into an office. They're going to fire me. Can I even *be* fired? *Shit, Shit, Shit.*

Dante storms into the room, his muscles straining under his murderous glare. It's hard, calculated, and deadly. I suck in a breath, preparing myself for his wrath. Sienna doesn't even send me an apologetic glance as she quickly scurries out of the room, leaving us alone.

I cross my arms over my chest. My lips are pursed as Dante and I have a stare down. "What the hell are you doing, Dante?"

His eyes narrow at my question. "What am I doing?" He laughs. "First, no one disrespects my girls, ever. You were trying to get up and he wasn't letting you. Second, your job is to serve. We have a hierarchy here. You are at the bottom, learning your way to the top."

"You said yourself, the tips I make are mine to keep. TJ is a big tipper. I need that money. There was no reason for you to toss him out, and now..." I can't finish my sentence with the way Dante is staring at me with rage practically boiling in his eyes.

"You don't get special privileges because I used to know you once upon a time. This is business, Demi, and I won't tolerate anyone fucking with what I have created."

"The other girls told me..." I gasp at the sudden movement of Dante picking me up. He sits down in his large armchair and bends me over his lap. My shorts are torn off with an echoing rip, leaving my ass bare to him. He slaps me hard. His hand massages the area before he slaps me again. This time, it's his lips that soothe the light ache. When the sting disappears, it's replaced with desire. I'm slapped a third time.

Arousal pools between my legs. His hand grabs at my inner thigh and spreads them as his teeth scrape down my skin with little nips.

"Dante, what the hell?"

I try to sit up, embarrassed I like this way too much.

"You want to be treated this way? Then I'll treat you how you want. What do you think TJ wanted from you?"

His finger circles my wet entrance, moving my slickness to my clit. "You are *my* slut, Demi." He pushes his finger into me and I moan at the sudden intrusion. I feel his tongue on my skin and he moves toward my forbidden entrance. His tongue circles my puckered hole. The combination feels like heaven. I'm too into it to tell him to stop. A better version of me should.

My hips move to his rhythm without my permission. I'm almost dry humping his leg as he fingers me.

I'm so close to coming. I don't remember the last time I had an orgasm that I didn't cause myself.

"Are you going to disobey me again?" he asks, his fingers stopping. My hips keep moving craving that high Dante gives me.

"I didn't know I was disobeying you." His fingers refuse to move so I wiggle in his lap. "But I know now, and I'll try not to make the same mistake."

"Try?"

"I won't." I quickly say, and his fingers move again. His fingers fuck me while his other hand circles my other hole. He adds just a bit of pressure and I'm moaning out his name.

"Guaranteed, TJ wouldn't have made you come." He stands, pushing me off his lap, and walks out of the room, slamming the door after him.

What the hell just happened in here? I'm confused, mortified, and ashamed by how I reacted.

I pick up my shredded shorts that will no longer fit and I blow out an annoyed breath. My heart is still pounding like a drum when the door opens a crack. I run behind the desk to seek cover and watch as a female arm slips in, placing a pair of Throne of Sin shorts just inside the door.

After stepping into the new shorts, I walk out on shaky legs. I can't help but look for Dante. He's nowhere in sight.

"What happened? I've never seen Dante look so mad," Robin asks. I give her a fake smile, still unsure what to say, and shrug.

"If I were you, I would bust my ass tonight. If Dante comes back and you're not working your share, I'd hate to see what would happen."

"I have to ask..." I don't know why I'm even going here... "How many people in this room have slept with Dante?"

"Oh, girl, don't be giving him those big savior eyes. Our work conditions are fair. It's why no one ever leaves, but Dante doesn't mix business with pleasure. If you are already one of his girls, he will never touch you. He doesn't sample the merchandise, if you know what I'm saying."

"Drinks are ready," Sienna calls toward us as a not-so-subtle way to make us stop talking and get back to work.

Robin dips her head and whispers, "She's mean. Don't get on her nasty side." She walks away in the opposite direction without a backward glance. Robin is the girl who walks around to do lap dances. Sometimes she takes the men into a curtained off area while others are in a back room. I stand, watching as she works the room with a confidence I don't think I'll ever have.

"Demi!" Sienna shouts and points toward a tray of drinks. I go toward the bar, trying to get my head back into the game.

"That girl is the queen of gossip. Be careful around her." As a general rule, I make a habit out of trusting no one. Everyone screws me one way or the other and I end up on the bottom. I nod at Sienna's advice and give her a fake smile before grabbing my tray.

I look at the ticket that says what table they go to and continue serving drinks, making sure I don't make any unwelcome eye contact with anyone. I really need this job and I can't have Dante tossing me out.

Chapter 9

Dante

Sienna keeps casting glances at me like she wants to ask a question. I sip on my water, looking over the floor of the club while pretending to do paperwork to avoid any conversation. The folders are spread in front of me, but they refuse to hold my interest. Instead, my eyes want to stay glued to Demi in her corset and booty shorts. I've never hated my dress code until now. She should have more clothes on. Too many of the men are looking at her like a piece of meat. I scoff at the thought, Demi is already the most conservatively dressed out of everyone.

"I've never seen you like this before." My head turns to the side to find Sienna standing there with a wide smile.

I grunt a noncommittal response and open a folder. She doesn't leave and laughs while placing a hand on my shoulder. Automatically, I roll my shoulder to remove her hand. I hate people touching me. She does it to push my buttons and see how far she can go.

"The customers love her and she's efficient but you won't be able to keep her as a waitress for long. She wants to earn more money," Sienna mentions, going back behind the bar, wiping the counters. I can't tell if she's telling me this to mock me, or truly letting me know the predicament I have on my hands.

"The only thing money will do is send her back to whatever addiction she is fighting," I scoff but, like a magnet, my eyes find her immediately. She's beautiful.

"I don't get the impression she does drugs."

I close the folder and look at Sienna again. "Then why does she need money badly enough that she came *here* for work? She has no bills."

"What did she say when you asked her?"

My eyes narrow into a glare. "Sweet, innocent girls don't get sold at auctions. It's always their past demons that send them to me. She'll be no different."

"Maybe I'm looking at her past demon?"

My head snaps back. "What the fuck does that mean?" I haven't told anyone that Demi and I have history.

She raises her hand in surrender. "Simmer down. I was only implying that you must know her since she asked for a job first, but now you've piqued my interest." She walks away having the last word.

If Sienna wasn't so great at her job, I'd fire her.

Demi doesn't make it back to my office until three AM. She walks in and falls into the leather armchair I had spanked her on earlier. She slips off her shoes and rubs at her feet. I can't stop staring and my fingers itch to grab her foot and do it for her. Instead, I stay focused on sitting behind my desk.

"Why am I staying with you when all the other girls live in a house together?" she asks.

I can't stand the thought of being away from you. "I'm still seeing if you can be trusted," I reply in a bored, annoyed tone, trying to seem indifferent. I hate the way she gets under my skin without trying.

"The girls are seeing it as me getting special treatment. They also don't understand why I'm not doing lap dances or dancing on stage yet."

"Is this your way of saying you want to rub yourself on some dirty old man and live with a bunch of mean girls?"

She slips off her other shoe. "I'm the outsider. These girls see themselves as family and look out for one another. They'll never accept me until I'm being treated like they are."

"Fine, you can dance twice a week. I'll tell Sienna to place you on the schedule. We'll see how much they like it when two of them lose a shift on stage."

She leans back, crossing her arms, and glares at me. "The girls on stage get to do private dances if requested."

"Fine, but only in room two." My answer leaves an acid taste in my mouth and my fingers curl around the edge of my desk.

"Why room two?"

"Because it has a two-way mirror so I can make sure you are giving the quality my club is known for." My spit flies to the edge of my desk as I talk. I need to learn to control my emotions around this girl.

My pulse quickens at the thought of anyone touching her. It's so unlike me. I'm the guy who prefers to watch. It goes with my whole no touching thing. But with Demi, I'm transported back to when I was a teen who didn't have those types of issues.

"You and your brothers are a waste of space." My mother stands over me and uses her foot to nudge me.

"Did you poison me?" I ask as I unleash another round into the toilet. I'm going to die, I just know it. My stomach cramps, I'm sweaty and cold, every muscle throbs.

"Don't be dramatic. You have the flu."

She laughs, walking out of the room as I lie on the cold ceramic tile. Its once-square pieces are cracked, some edges missing entirely. I'm curled in on myself, fading in and out of consciousness. I can hear my mother in my room, but I can't bring myself to care. I'm too tired.

"You actually think that girl next door looks at you like you're worth anything?" I don't know when she came back or how long she's been there, but my mother is crouched down to my level and I see she has Demi's ring in her hands. "You are a stupid boy."

I attempt to sit up, my muscles screaming in protest. She shoves the ring in my mouth, placing a hand over my lips as she hits me with her cross over my arm and back. Its sharp points dig into my skin and it doesn't take long before my body opens up to the beating.

"You need to go to church, boy."

When she's out of breath, she leaves. I keep the ring in my mouth, scared she'll do something with it.

When I wake up next, a cold object is running over my skin. I sit up, placing my hand out to strangle my mother. My fingers grip her neck.

"It's me, Dante! Demi."

My grip releases automatically and I fall back down with a groan.

"I got you. You sleep and I'll protect you."

I roll to my knees, using the toilet as a stool to help me stand. When my back is turned, I slip the ring out of my mouth and into my pocket. Demi places her small frame under my arm as I limp toward my bed.

She places a cold compress on my forehead, making it feel better than it should. I pull my handgun out from under my pillow. "If she comes back, shoot the bitch, and I'll say I did it."

Demi doesn't say anything while she continues to clean me up. I guess she knows where I got my scars now.

"How many people know about this two-way mirror?" My head tilts back at the surprise in Demi's voice, it brings me back to the present.

It's another reminder we're not the same people we used to be. She's staring at me expectantly. Yes, *the two-way mirror room and who knows about it.*

"It's normal protocol and everyone knows about it. In fact, many take it as an honor to be in that room."

"Okay then, thank you." She slips her shoes back on but her whole face scrunches up like it hurts worse than it did before.

I lean to the side and toss a pair of sandals at her. "Wear these."

When I'm trying to be more casual, I wear them myself, but that never happens. Her feet are swallowed by the large leather thongs. It's almost comical. "The other option is I carry you out of here. In front of everyone."

She laughs and it does something strange to my heart. "No, I don't need the girls talking about me more than they already do."

My fists curl into themselves. I'll have Sienna deal with this problem. "Let's go home." I stand and walk out of the room. It takes everything in me not to pick her up and throw her over my shoulder. She limps slightly with each step. The last of the girls are sitting at a table, counting their tips for the night. I give them a wave.

When the cool night air wraps itself around me, I pick up Demi, despite her demanding I put her down.

"I can't have you limping at work tomorrow. It's bad for business," I grunt.

Her womanly scent swirls around me, still the same as all those years ago. I place her on the passenger seat and buckle her in myself.

Chapter 10

Demi

THIS IS THE FIRST night I've worked without Dante in the club. I can't stop watching the entrance for his arrival.

"What has her so distracted tonight?" One of the other girls, Tanya, asks.

I turn and Robin answers. "She's obviously watching for Dante. I tried to tell her he never goes for girls like us."

"You both are wrong." I roll my eyes, annoyed how they're talking about me like I'm not here. It's comical watching their eyebrows raise in question.

"I'm just saying, I've been here for five years. If Demi so much as thinks about trying to climb the corporate ladder via his cock, I'm going to have issues," Tanya responds, glaring at me like I'm a cockroach that she would love to squish with her foot.

I grab my tray, happy to get away from them, and walk around the room to deliver the glasses to their owners. I can't help but notice the other girls watching me out of the corners of their eyes. It unsettles me. I've been out-of-my-way nice to them, and still, I'm an outsider. If I'm going to fit in, I have to jump in with both feet and Dante can't have me at his place anymore.

"I heard she's still not allowed to do lap dances." Tanya is talking to another girl, both of them staring at me while she speaks.

"I wonder what he would do if he found her banging a client." They giggle as I set my empty tray down.

"I can do whatever the hell I want." I practically spit at them. Turning to Sienna, I call out my next order.

"The most successful girls here fuck. It's how I can afford my penthouse. Once your debt is paid, you don't have to live in communal living anymore." I thought they all lived together. "Don't worry, one day you'll have your training chastity panties removed." Shelby smirks and her shoulder pushes against me as she walks away.

I've never been popular. I always liked to stick to myself because of assholes like these girls.

"So, what's the gossip of the day, ladies?" Dante's voice sends shivers down my spine. The other two girls immediately straighten, their giggles vanishing before they get back to work.

I keep my eyes forward, my face slowly heating as I wait for my drinks.

"What the hell was that about?" Dante asks in a low, rumbly voice.

"Just a little shop talk." I plaster on a fake smile, wishing Sienna would hurry the hell up with my order.

"Why the blush then?"

This is mortifying, and if I plan to get these girls to accept me, I can no longer be seen using Dante as a crutch. I have to stop talking to him so much.

His hand rests on top of mine and we both look at it before he lets it slide back to his side. Sienna places the drinks on my tray and I turn away, running off to drop off the glasses. I can feel his eyes sear into my back as he watches me, but I refuse to look over my shoulder.

"Word of advice?" I turn to see Tanya again. I'm really beginning to dislike this chick. "The customers need to know you're available. The moment they think Dante has claim on you, they will never fuck you, want a dance, or even buy a drink from you."

"Last time I checked, this club isn't a whorehouse. We do lap dances and that's all." Dante's angry face flashes into my mind. Like he said, over his dead body would he allow me to sell my body.

"You really are sweet and innocent." She looks around and lowers her voice. "Keep that going for you; you'll have the men eating out of the palm of your hand."

Shelby steps up, adding, "If that is the case, why the monthly testing for STIs? Last I checked, dancing doesn't get you any type of sexually transmitted disease. And what about the mandatory IUD?"

I stand there stupidly because Dante hasn't brought this up to me yet. It's another thing they can use against me.

"Dante is going to keep his thumb on you at all times. You might feel special right now, but I'm getting out of here. You'll be here for the rest of your life," Tanya cockily retorts.

I've had enough. My hip sways into her as I walk away, but she's wormed her way into my head. She's right. I need to do more to get my daughter faster and Dante gave me the green light to do lap dances.

I go back to the bar, sliding Sienna my new list of drinks. Robin is waiting for her next tray too. She's the one I feel most comfortable asking. "Have you ever had sex with a client?"

She looks around before whispering into my ear. "Never without a condom. No matter what they offer to pay." She takes her drinks and disappears.

I guess this *is* a regular thing.

I lick my lips, which are suddenly extremely dry. Just the thought of sleeping with clients brings up so many memories of my past.

"You okay?" I glance up at Sienna and force a smile.

"Of course." I give her a shrug.

The tray seems to be a hundred pounds heavier than before. I don't understand why Dante has placed a double standard for me.

"Thanks, Demi." I hand the last drink on my tray out to a table full of men in suits. "How much for a dance for my friend here?"

"You know the price, Leon, and don't you dare try to barter on it," Robin comes to my rescue. I don't even know what the protocol for this is. Maybe I should have asked Dante before I demanded I be allowed.

I'm still lost in my thoughts when Robin adds, "Price is upfront. Cash. Then she'll come back with a room number."

"Are you as bossy as she is?" the guy who's getting the lap dance asks.

"One way to find out." Robin has completely taken over the conversation for me. I'm grateful for it. The man hands her cash and she passes it to me.

"We'll be back," I say, following Robin.

"We need a key," she tells Sienna.

Sienna holds out her hand and I place the crisp new bills in her hand. "I hold the money to keep it safe. You get it at the end of the night. This way you're not robbed." I nod, and she places a key in my hand. "Boss man say you were allowed?"

"Yes." I straighten my back. Slowly, I get control of my head and confidence.

I walk back to Leon's table. He's in his mid-fifties, by the look of it. My eyes narrow in on the plain gold band on his hand. My stomach swooshes. *I need the money.*

"I was afraid you were going to change your mind," he says, standing. "What room?"

"Two," I answer, and he chuckles under his breath. It makes me self-conscious.

"You really are a newbie. Or is it that Dante has a thing for you?" he asks from behind me, his breath hitting my neck. I place the key into the lock and his front touches my back. "I know his kink is to watch. We'll have to make sure to give him a show worth watching."

"What?" We step into the room and he closes the door. My heart thunders a mile a minute.

"He likes a good show. We don't want to disappoint him." Leon nods toward the two-way mirror. I swallow down the saliva collecting in my mouth.

Music starts up the moment the door is closed and the lights dim themselves. Leon walks over to the couch, leaving me standing by the pole in the room.

My hand wraps around the metal to keep me steady.

"Do a little dance to warm both of us up." He sinks back into the couch and rubs himself for a second. My stomach turns. *I can do this. I have to do this.*

I drop to my knees and pop up, allowing my butt to be in the air as I take my time moving upward. The entire time, my eyes shift between the man on the couch and the mirror.

"You like having the audience too, I see." He leers at me, his grin almost sadistic. Or maybe it's all in my head. "Bring that delicious ass toward me."

I grip the pole tighter and my feet shuffle as I try a different routine. I wiggle my ass, trying to get lost in my dancing. It's time Dante learns he can't treat me differently. In my mind, I'm dancing for Dante, even though he's probably not watching.

"We both know dancing on that thing is not your strong suit. Show me what your talent really is."

I take the scrunchy from my hair and allow my ponytail to drop. With a shake, my long locks float to the middle of my back.

"No touching." I wrap my elastic around his hands. He could free himself easily enough if he wanted to, but he adjusts himself and I can tell he's liking this. I don't think I could go through with it if he touched me.

I seductively sway my hips over to Leon. I make a show of lifting my leg easily above my head and turn so my back is facing him.

With the beat to the song I lower myself, bending in half when his pants hit my leg. I move up and down, shaking my ass.

His fingers untie my corset and the ribbon slacks against my skin. Turning, I cage him so my breasts and his face are the same height.

He pulls me in closer and I fall into a straddle over him. I don't want to be here. When I left town, I vowed I'd never find myself in a situation like my mother used to place me in. But look at me now; I've come full circle, because I demanded it.

The door opens with a bang and I'm pulled off the couch. Dante's scent wraps around me.

"You need to leave. Now," he growls.

"I expect my money back and a free dance."

"You're going to get my fist in your face if you don't walk away in three seconds."

My fingers reach behind me and quickly do up the ribbons, securing my top. Dante is breathing hard, the cords in his neck straining.

The music is cut short, its silence making the room thick with tension.

I stand, placing my hands on my hips. "You said I could dance!"

He stalks toward me. "Dance, not fuck. The rules haven't changed Demi. If you need to fuck someone it will be me. It has always been me." His nostrils flare while he cracks one knuckle at the time until he towers over me.

His hands sweep behind me and undo the ribbon. His dark irises lock on me, daring me to do something about it.

"I wasn't going to fuck him."

The pads of his fingers brush against my skin. My face heats, and I feel my flush creep from my neck to my cheeks. "No. You wanted to fuck with me. That's why you kept watching the mirror."

His hand stops moving in circles on my back.

"Let's go home." He sighs.

"I have a shift to finish." I refuse to move.

"No you don't. I just cut you. From now on, you will serve and dance on stage. That's it."

"Dante, you can't be serious."

"I'm deadly serious. Next time, I'll make you watch me shoot the next guy you touch. Then I'll fuck you over their dead body. Do I make myself clear?"

I use all my might to shove at his chest, but he doesn't move. "Careful, the night's young and this is turning into foreplay for me," he growls.

I step to the side to walk past him, but he picks me up, swinging my upper body over his shoulder, and smacks my ass. He walks out the side door and we leave the club.

Chapter 11

Dante

I SHOULD HAVE MURDERED Leon the second I tossed him out of the club. *The night's still young.* I walk into my house and head straight for my bedroom. Demi fights me each step of the way. My cock grows harder with her small fists punching at my back.

I drop her on my bed and her small frame bounces twice before she's standing up and poking at my solid chest.

"I'm a grown adult, and you need to start treating me like everyone else."

"I love that idea," I sneer. I walk into my bathroom and look at the stuff I use to help people lose consciousness.

"This is your plan? Poison me to make me agreeable? You're more like your mother than you think."

Her words hit me square in the chest.

"I don't need to sedate you to control you, Demi." My eyes narrow in on hers, but she refuses to cower. She straightens her spine, like she's preparing herself for war.

"You'll stay in this room with me from now on," I demand, studying her reaction. Her stunning emerald eyes flare to life as they narrow in on mine. "You can't be trusted and I need to keep a better eye on you," I lie. I'm tired of her sleeping in another room. I crave her presence even when I hate myself for it. "You want to be treated like one of my whores, so be it."

I let out a sharp whistle that makes her jump and my doctor walks in. Her eyes widen and I don't miss the fear that coats her irises, but it quickly disappears.

"This is my doctor. He's here to give you an STI screening and pregnancy test."

Her legs twist off the bed and a moment later, she's on her feet, marching toward me. "My own doctor gave me a physical last year. I have no need for another one."

"I own you. You *will* have another one." We face off with one another.

The doctor clears his throat. "I can wait…"

I cut him off. "I'll wait outside while you do your thing. Unless you want me to be in the room, Demi."

She glares at me, her eyes feeling like they could shoot a hundred daggers into my soul. "I don't need you in here," she replies angrily.

I nod, placing my hands behind my back. My legs are stiff as I control my movements to be calm and slow. When I close the door behind me, I want to kick myself for even giving her the option. I should have stayed with her. I pace the outside of the room, my instincts demanding I barge back in, but I try to stay calm.

The doctor comes out a few minutes later. "Did you want me to come back to insert the IUD?"

"No. She's not going to need one of those."

We shake hands and I reenter my room.

"You moved my clothes into your room?" She's opening and shutting my dresser doors.

That didn't take her long to find out. "What were you hoping to find when you went snooping?" Her little outburst is comical. She slams the drawer shut and turns to face me.

"Snooping? HA! I saw those stupid lace panties you force me to wear hanging out!"

"I hardly force you. I don't mind if you wear none."

She blinks twice at me, not saying a word, before she raises her voice. "Stop showing me favoritism! I can't be living here with you." She goes to one of her drawers, pulling it out, and dumping its contents on the floor with a thud.

I bite on my lower lip, not commenting, refusing to give her anything other than a bored facial expression.

"Do we feel better after that tantrum?" I ask, hating the mess she created.

"I don't want your concern!"

My control snaps. I grab her chin, not to hurt her, but to force her to look at me. "Do not yell at me. I am not a child. When you behave like an adult, I will consider you moving out. Until then, you will live under my roof."

"Is this a Daddy kink you have? Should I be saying, 'yes, daddy' every time you bark a demand at me?" she replies sweetly. Too sweetly. She steps in closer and smiles. "First, it's spankings, and now this."

Every trace of sweetness leaves her body without warning and she stomps on my foot.

A growl vibrates deep within my chest. "I have no interest in being your daddy. This is business and you're costing me money."

I tug her closer and find that her heart is beating as fast as mine against my chest. I want to kiss her, rip her clothes off her and see if she feels as fantastic as she did ten years ago. Demi is mine and I'll never let her go. Soon enough, she will come to the same conclusion.

"I have a function to go to this month. You'll come with me as my plus one." I never bring a date to these things, but I have a feeling Demi will be perfect for the role.

"Like Hell I will." She pushes off me. This time I allow her the space.

"This isn't how it works. I tell you you're going to do something and you say yes." I turn around, needing to distance myself before I slam my lips against hers.

She makes the mistake of grabbing my arm. "We're not done talking."

I lift a brow, feeling myself harden as she attempts to assert herself. "I'll buy you a dress and you will plaster a happy smile on your face. You will look like the pretty trophy you are on my arm and stay silent. That's your job. If you open your mouth one more time, I'll put my cock in it until you learn your place."

She glances up at me and, for a split second, I think the old lust that used to shine for me surfaces. *It has to be in my imagination.* I have always been her white knight but never her prince. She's here because she needs something from me. I stare her down a moment longer, daring her to say another word. My dick throbs in my pants, wanting to come out and play with Demi one more time.

I flick my hand away, jerking free of her grasp. I'm disgusted with myself. This is the problem every time I get close to her. I always want more than what she can give.

"Your shift starts at eight tonight," I reply, trying to disengage myself from caring too much. "Don't forget my door is open if you need to whore yourself out."

She sucks in a breath of air. My comment was meant to hurt *her* so why does it feel like *I'm* the one who got punched in the gut?

I leave her to herself and silently close the door as I try to calm my racing heart.

Chapter 12

Demi

A FEW HOURS LATER, I'm walking ten feet in front of Dante as we enter the club. He refused my suggestion that we show up separately, stating this is his club, he can do whatever he wants. Each of the girls follow my strides with their hidden looks as I make my way further in. Their eyes burn with jealousy and disgust for me.

Even Robin doesn't come to say hello as fast as she normally does.

"What's with everyone tonight?" I ask Sienna, even though I know.

She shrugs. "I'm used to it. They used to pull shit like that with me when I first started."

"How much is your debt?" I can't help but wonder what the average length of time is that a girl stays here.

"Oh, I'm here of my own free will. Dante has never owned me but, like everyone else, I needed saving, and Dante was there for me. I love this job. There has never been a reason for me to leave."

I turn, leaning against the bar, and watch the girl on stage. I study her moves, hoping I can at least do a good job at that, and without Dante ripping me from the stage.

"We have never seen anything like this before. You show up, and two of our top customers get thrown out. The others are blaming you for the shortage of tips."

My stomach drops and I feel horribly guilty. "I'm sorry about that, but it's not my fault. I had no control over what happened to them," I defend myself.

"Mmmkay. Just saying, you're the only person I know who gets under Dante's skin like that." Sienna continues to make drinks as she talks to me.

I can only imagine what they'll say when they hear I'm going to be his date for an event.

"Hey, Dem," Robin interrupts before turning to Sienna. "I need a room." She hands the cash over to Sienna.

"Room three, Robin." Sienna places a key into her hand and Robin goes on her way.

"Fifteen minutes until you're up," Sienna dismisses me.

The locker room is vacant, leaving me to my thoughts as I strip out of my clothes and stand in my bra and panties. My feet shuffle toward the mirror, taking in my appearance. The markings on my stomach draw my eyes to them, creating a new bundle of nerves that set into my muscles. My stretch marks rake against my skin; white stripes, painting their canvas into an imperfect blemish. I dig into my bag, opening up my makeup, and apply a layer of coverup. The indent markings are still there, but they'll blend in better under the bright light.

Opening my locker, a new stage outfit hangs inside with the tags still on. The material is soft and feels expensive. It's another thing for the girls to judge me on. Without a thought, I toss the new clothing into the trash and pull out the clothes I had originally picked. This outfit, unlike the one I found, will cover my stomach until I need to take it off.

I add a touch more makeup to my face, changing my lips from nude to bright red. Between my face and my breasts I hope they're enough to draw the attention away from my stomach. None of the other girls have stretch marks, or kids for that matter. At least, not that I'm aware of.

My heart squeezes, missing my daughter. I miss her face, her sweet voice, and those perfect hugs she gives. I'm not sure how long I can stay away from her. The distance is killing me.

"We all know you're going to choke once you get on stage." I turn to see Tanya. She seems to be the ringleader of how all the other girls act around me.

"Probably." I shrug, trying to think of a way to make friends with this woman. I walk around the lockers toward the mirror and retrieve the outfit I had thrown out. "We all know I could learn a thing or two. Any tips for me?" I ask as I round the corner and hand her the outfit. "This is for you."

She eyes me up and down and I attempt to kill her with kindness. "Dante needs a date for an event later in the month." Tanya and I are about the same build, she would fit whatever dress Dante buys me. Maybe this could help forge a friendship between the two of us. "You can go in my place and use the dress he sends."

"He never takes any of us girls to events." She flicks her hair over her shoulder, trying to mask her excitement at the prospect.

"Maybe I heard wrong."

"Take your time with getting rid of layers. The men like the chase," she finally says. I can't help but think that I'm one step closer to maybe having an ally. When she goes out with Dante, all the girls will be forced to accept me.

"I'll remember that."

I look in the mirror one last time before I hear the song end, signaling my turn. My pulse increases, but I'm not afraid. I'm excited about showing everyone that I can handle this job. My entire life, I've always had to prove myself. This energy I'm feeling is the same I always get before I prove to everyone I can do as well as them.

I walk on stage and there are two guys in the front row, but they're talking to each other. The tables are busy and everyone is in conversation. Disappointment that there isn't more attention on the stage tries to wiggle its way in, but it's completely forgotten when I see Dante at the bar having a drink.

His eyes come to life seeing me in my outfit and it spurs me on to walk with confidence. Grabbing the pole in the middle of the stage, I walk around it, maneuvering my body to have the pole at my back. My knees dip and I glance over at Dante again.

His facial features are hard as he takes a sip of the colorless liquid in his short glass. A few of the waitresses cat-call toward the stage, giving me more confidence. I shake my ass and allow the strap of my dress to fall down my arm.

A few of the men in the room look up and their attention locks on my dancing. My leg hooks around the pole and I let the momentum carry me into a twirl before allowing my other strap to slide down my arm. While I dance, I seductively lower my dress until I can drop it off. I'm wearing a bra that outlines my breasts, my boobs stick out of it for all to see, and the material clings to my skin as it dips toward my hips. My panties are sheer, and the material spiders over my ass, showing my skin off.

A glass breaking catches my attention and I can't help but smirk when I see that Dante's glass has slipped from his fingers. The grooves in his forehead dip between his eyes and my body continues to move to the song, but I'm unable to take my eyes off him. Why would he be so angry with me dancing? Or is it something else?

It takes all of my effort to tear my concentration away from him and focus on the crowd. I have the whole room's attention, but it's Dante's burning gaze that has my skin prickling into goosebumps. I continue my dance, thriving on the energy in the room. On stage, I feel beautiful and talented.

After my set is done, the girls pat me on the back, congratulate me, or at least give me a smile. I finally feel like, just maybe, I've broken through an invisible wall with them. The entire experience has me smiling. I don't remember the last time I didn't have to force a smile. Some of the weight resting on my shoulders lifts, but it's impossible to be completely free when I know I still have to find a way to get back to my daughter as soon as possible.

Dante

I can't sit here and watch every male's eye on Demi. My fingers keep curling into fists and all I want to do is drag her down from the stage. The need to punch every man's gawking face festers inside of me.

"Why does he look like he's about to go on a murdering spree?" I jump at the sound of Maximus's voice.

"Shouldn't you be dismantling a body somewhere?" Sienna asks, leaning over the counter, placing her tits on full display.

I look between them. They seem friendly. *Too friendly.*

"Sienna doesn't mix pleasure with business. Stop looking at her," I scold.

Sienna immediately straightens and I grab my brother's shoulder, pushing him toward my office.

"What the hell are you doing here?" I ask, closing my door.

"Savio seems to think there's some type of threat coming from within the club. Something about an IP address." He shrugs, scratching at his cheek before taking a seat. "Why are you in a shitty mood? Does it have something to do with your girlfriend stripping?"

I count to three before I answer. My nostrils flare, but I refuse to react. "She's the new girl." It's all I'm going to give him.

He grunts. "You and Sienna together, then?"

An amused chuckle escapes me. "No." She's like the little sister I never had.

"Then why are you cock blocking me?"

My head cocks to the side, my lips pursing. "This is my business. I'm not letting family get in the way of it. I have a 'no fucking my family' rule."

"Okay. I can work with that. Romeo wants me to hang around for a little to see what's happening, if that's okay with you. I don't want to be stepping on your toes or anything."

I wave his concern away. "No, I'm fine with that. I want what's best for the family."

"Good. Then we agree." He extends his hand and shakes mine.

Chapter 13

Demi

Dante is silent on the way back to his house. There's a thick tension that continues to coil around us in his car but I don't dare say anything about it, scared of the outburst—when he finally explodes. He opens his car door, and I do the same. Intentionally, I stay a few feet behind him as I follow into the house.

I roll my shoulders, hoping to make them feel less tight. My arms aren't used to the workout the club's pole gave them.

Dante goes to his counter and pulls out a bottle of scotch. This is my cue to leave. Memories of my father, drunk and bellowing, force me to walk away.

I head into Dante's room, taking off my clothes before I put on a silk robe and pad back through the massive house. Dante is sitting in the dark on a large brown leather throne-like chair. I turn the other direction toward the back door. Slipping through the glass door, I head toward the red lights illuminating the hot tub.

My robe slips from my shoulders and I allow it to fall to the ground. I dip one foot in first, the sudden warmth sending a prickling sensation through my toes. I add a second foot, waiting for the pins and needles to leave before I walk the rest of the way in.

The warmth cocoons me and I let out a long sigh, dropping my head back on the edge of the tub. This is what I need. It's been a long time since I've felt heat like this.

My thoughts drift to my daughter. I've never gone this long without seeing or talking to her. I hope she's doing okay. My eyes drift up the length of the grand building. When Dante and I used to talk about running away, I always envisioned somewhere small and cozy. He always wanted to open the universe for me. Looks like he got part of his wish.

"Remember how we used to wish on stars?" Dante's voice sounds from the dark before I see him walk closer.

"Looks like you got everything you hoped you would." I answer, allowing my eyes to drift shut once more.

"Why did you search me out?" he asks. His voice is closer and I can hear him take a sip of his drink.

"Not tonight, Dante. I'm too exhausted."

"Don't you think I deserve some type of explanation?"

I open my eyes, looking at him. "I promise we'll have that talk, but not tonight."

He sets his drink down on the ledge. "Hand me your foot." His hand dips into the water as I lift my left foot. His hands massage my sore and tired arches.

"How the hell are you this nice *and* in the mafia?"

His hands stop moving and I lift my other foot. "I *am* the guy people warn you about. Don't mistake my kindness for something it's not. I buy women for a living. I own a strip club. You are an investment."

I should fear him, but my heart refuses to allow me. Right now, we are Dante and Demi from across the street.

"What about the mafia part? How did that happen? Last I checked, you were just another poor kid from across the street."

"My brother, Romeo, is the Mancini Don. He's much older than me. He took Savio and I in when we went looking for him."

"Family business, lucky guy."

"We had to earn our keep, just like everyone else. Romeo doesn't play favorites. I wasn't handed anything for free. I worked my ass off for all of this." His fingers dig into the pads of my feet as he gets worked up.

I allow for my body to sink under the surface, removing my foot from his hold. I bask in the warmth of the water before I resurface and wipe my hands down my face as I blow my breath out.

Dante is gone by the time I clear my vision, leaving me with only the hulking shadows of the house as company.

I climb out of the tub when I can't take the heat anymore and wrap the silk robe around me, not caring that it will soon be soaked with water. My skin steams into the night air as I walk into the house.

There's no sign of Dante as I step into the house and I can't help but wonder if he went out. The other girls often talk about his famous parties he hosts when his brother, Savio, fights in the cages. Did Savio fight tonight and he's off hosting a party at some club?

I'm forced to turn on a few lights as I make my way back to the bedroom. When I open the door, Dante is lying on his back, asleep in bed. His cocktail, only half drank, rests on the side table.

I step into the dim room, the only light coming from the hallways, and walk into the closet. I opt for one of Dante's old sweaters. It's thin and has holes in one of the arms. I slip it over my cooling skin and breathe his scent in. I use the robe to dry off my legs and move back into the hallway, leaving Dante asleep.

All I can think about is calling Oakleigh. I miss her incredibly. It hurts my heart every time I think about leaving her. I have to talk to her. I glance back into the room to make sure Dante really *is* sleeping before I make my way to the phone farthest from him.

I walk toward his office in the dark, casting a look over my shoulder when my hand touches the knob. My hand twists, and it opens without problem. I hustle behind his desk, opening drawers one after another until I see a cellphone. A small gray flip phone rests inside. I pick it up, discovering it's dead and won't turn on. Shuffling a few things over I look for a plug in cord with no success.

My hands place on my hips, and I know Dante always carries a phone on him. My heart speeds up at my idea. Returning to the room, my eyes are heavy. The glass of liquid still sits untouched, shining in the hallway light as if in a spotlight. Beside it is his gun...and a cell phone.

How did I miss that?

My heart skips a beat as I close the door to the frame, not wanting to make a sound. I walk toward Dante until my legs hit the bed, and I stop, listening for his even breathing.

I take a few steps farther and come to a stop by his head. He looks the same as all those years ago when he sleeps. The hardened lines etched into his features have softened, allowing a shadow of his younger self to come through.

My hand hovers over the gun. It's not like that would help me. I move past it, picking up the phone and slipping it into the kangaroo pocket in front. I pick up his drink and bring it to my lips.

An Old Fashioned by the smell of it. It goes down smooth. Stepping just out into the hall, I quickly dial my mother's old number. I don't even know if she still has it or not. If she's been anything like me, she wouldn't be able to afford to keep a cell phone consistently.

It rings once, twice, three times. It was silly to even hold out hope. On the fifth ring, I get an answer. "Hello?" It's my mother's tired, scratchy voice.

"Sorry to wake you."

She scoffs, hearing my voice. "We can't all stay up late into the night. I'm raising your child and need to be responsible."

My molars grind, wanting to spit out a comeback, but I refuse. I didn't call to pick a fight. I crack open the door to check on Dante again. Still sleeping.

"I need another thousand Demi."

My heart plummets. "Why? Hasn't money been delivered to you in the last month?"

"The prescription was expensive. I could only get a few days' worth."

"You didn't get all the medication? Those drugs are very important." The heat from the hot tub has worn off and my skin prickles with goosebumps, my body shaking with the new chill racing though me.

"I tried." She doesn't sound like she's tried. All I ever wanted was for her to care but she has never given a shit; not then and not now.

"Well, try harder. That has to be enough."

A throat clearing has me screaming and jumping. Dante is leaning on the doorframe in his boxers. I quickly end the call, hiding his cell behind my back. His hand is already out in a silent request for the phone to be placed in his palm.

"Prescription drugs. I should have known you would be classier and not get involved with street stuff."

"I don't do drugs. Any type." I cross my arms, refusing to cower under his stare.

He lifts the phone from my fingers and presses the number I just called. I jump into action, taking the phone. "Fine, you found me out. I like to use them to take the edge off sometimes. It's no big deal."

"It is a big fucking deal. My girls are clean and don't do drugs. Look at you shake. You're going through withdrawal. Fuck, Demi." His hand swipes through his hair.

"I just need a second and my shaking will stop."

"It doesn't work that way. Have you ever tried to quit cold turkey before?"

"I'll be fine. Trust me."

Dante takes a step toward me and I take a step back. His look is cold and calculated as his proximity forces me back until I hit the wall. I flinch as he moves incredibly fast, his forearms hitting the wall. The sound loud, as if he punched it.

"You can't bully me into submission like you do to everyone else." I mumble under my breath, but I know he heard by the way his jaw ticks.

My body continues to tremble as he presses himself further into my space until we're practically touching from head to toe. All my emotions are knotted in the middle of my throat as the quiet noises of the settling house swirl around us.

Tick, tick...

The clock in the other room sounds like it's encroaching on us, breaking through the sound of our heavy breathing.

"What am I going to do with you?" His thumb and forefinger feather across my throat, as if he's testing to see if it fits. He applies pressure, not enough to hurt or block my airway, just enough to tell me he's the one in charge. When he brushes against my pulse, a small smirk lifts his lips.

My nipples strain, pushing against Dante's sweater.

"I should rip my shirt off you, bend you over, and teach you a lesson."

I rub my legs together, liking the way his voice and power turns me on.

What is wrong with me?

He laughs, sounding out of control, like he's about to snap. His hand sweeps down my throat, over my puckered nipple, and continues down my belly until he hits the naked flesh of my thigh.

"You're one breath away from being a psychopath." The defiance in my voice surprises even me.

He grips my hips, pressing himself into me. His thick erection has my clit tingling, wanting him to play with it. There's a raw hunger in his eyes that pins me in place. I'm drawn to his darkness like a moth to a flame. I want all the evil promises I know he's thinking but isn't brave enough to speak aloud.

He's always had a way of making me forget my problems, welcoming me into a world where nothing matters but him and me. The consequences could be worse than death and I'd still always go to him. I can't help it. When he's around, all rational thoughts dissipate. It's only after that I realize I've been burned from playing with fire.

His fingers slip under the material and glide over the outside of my pussy. His smile grows, feeling me wet for his touch.

"Your pussy craves my psychosis. You're one second away from falling to your knees and begging for my cock." My chest rises and falls against his. "You always take it like a good girl."

My legs shake and I place my hands against the wall behind me to help steady myself. "But tonight you've been a bad girl, and bad girls get nothing." He pushes himself off the wall and the loss of his touch has my skin turning cold. I'm left stunned and ashamed as he walks back into the bedroom.

"I'll give you five minutes to get your ass in bed, or else," he calls from in the room.

I breathe out, not understanding what just happened. My eyes instantly tear, and I wipe them away. Dante doesn't deserve my tears. He'll be lucky if I don't stab him while he sleeps.

"I can hear you over-thinking this, Demi. Get your ass to bed."

The roar of my pulse sounds like a river in my ears. I step back into the dark room, thankful there are no lights on. He lifts the covers for me, and I hesitate.

"One," he starts, and I don't want to find out what happens when he gets to three. I quickly slip under the blankets and pull them to my chin. "Good girl."

He pulls me in against his chest and all I can think about is the fact that I'm not wearing panties. Well, that and what has happened to Dante to make him change so much over the last decade. He's hot and cold and I never know what side of him I'm going to get. The littlest things seem to trigger this scary, demanding side of his. It's well into the night when my breathing finally becomes regular, and even longer until sleep pulls me under.

Thank goodness tomorrow is my day off.

Chapter 14

Dante

"Time to get up!" I lift the covers from Demi's gorgeous body. She groans, trying to steal the blankets back.

"It's my day off and I was awake all night."

"Not my problem."

"Dante," her voice has a bite to it and it has my lips curving upward. "Fuck off."

"Fine. When the girls get here, I'll just tell them you're still sleeping in my bed because you were up all night."

She sits up, glaring. "What girls?" She shoves her mangled locks out of her face.

"Savio is fighting tonight. I make the girls breakfast on the mornings of his big fights and they typically stick around to help with the party set up."

She huffs, getting out of bed. "I hate you right now." She rips off my old sweater, leaving her back to me, but she's fully naked. It's a sight to behold. My cock instantly perks up, wanting to follow her into the bathroom. I give in to its demand and do just that.

"What the hell are you doing?" she asks, seeing me on her tail. I take off my shirt and undo my belt.

"Taking a shower. What are you doing?" I ask innocently.

She waves a finger at me. "Oh, no you're not. I am." She tries to push me out of the way her small frame does nothing against my bulk. I shove down my pants and boxers in one go, leaving me naked in front of her.

"Oh, my God." She covers her eyes.

I lean into the crook of her neck. "I'm not shy, I don't mind if you look." She smells like chlorine and coconut. "Don't worry, I'll tell the girls you got really dirty and needed a shower when they get here."

Her soft growl sounds way too charming on her. She pulls out her scrunchy that's only holding half of her hair and her wild, dark locks fall clumsily past her shoulders. Time and age have made her more beautiful. Her hips have filled out and my fingers want to grip on to them. She leans over, turning on the water, her one leg rising with the motion.

I should never have followed her. Tormenting myself like this is stupid. I'm clearly not thinking with the right head. I need to keep her in a separate compartment and away from me. She looks over her shoulder and down at my erection. Her forehead lines grow deeper with her glare, her eyes trailing up my toned body, taking her time before she narrows them on mine.

I have to stop this cycle or I'll always be just the guy she turns to for help. She turns to face me, and the first thing I notice is the deep scar that runs across her lower stomach. The urge to pull her into me and ask about it is strong.

Don't do it.

I can't stop staring at it as she steps under the spray and closes her eyes, so I leave the room, slamming the door behind me.

I don't think she'd appreciate the cold shower that my body so desperately needs anyway.

Chapter 15

Demi

Dante stands overlooking the party in his backyard like a king. His forearms rest on the glass railing that fence in his balcony. Lights are strung above to cast a yellow glow. He surrounds himself with his brothers, Romeo, Max, and Savio. Sienna is there, too, but all the girls from the club are down on his stamped concrete patio, a clear sign we are below them. Once upon a time, I would have been up there with him.

I'm suddenly hit with an onslaught of sadness for what could have been. I should be up there with my best friend and our family. Instead, I'm surrounded by strangers. When I look back up, Dante is no longer looking down at us. He's probably sitting and enjoying his throne of sin. I think I understand why he named his club that.

I walk toward the girls, who are all talking in a circle. Tanya takes a step to the side to grab a drink and my eyes instantly spot Dante just behind. He's talking to a beautiful blonde while every other girl from the club eyes him, waiting to get his attention. He ignores them all, his attention solely on this woman. My stomach clenches and I'm overwhelmed with a feeling of jealousy. It's irrational. I have no claim on him.

I step closer, wanting to see who this lady is and why she's so special that he left his inner circle to mingle with us common folk. My feet keep going until I'm in the circle of club girls. I feel like a groupie and the thought has me stopping.

The woman laughs at what he's saying. Out of the corner of my eye, I study his face while trying to make it look like I haven't seen him yet. His features are relaxed, he's smiling, unlike every time he sees me. His smile is a panty dropper, it's the same one that caught my attention all those years ago. He's so handsome when he lets his guard down. Dante spots me and the hardened lines reappear on his face, his easy smile replaced with a forced one.

"Demi."

I tuck a piece of hair behind my ears, expecting to see jealousy and an angry scowl when the girl turns toward me. Instead, she steps up and gives me a hug, catching me by surprise.

"It's so nice to meet you," she says, holding the hug longer than is comfortable. I stand there with my arms at my sides, taken back by the warm welcome. "I'm Charlotte, Savio's wife."

Relief floods my nerves. Dante whispers something to her and she slaps him teasingly. That's when I see her ring glisten, catching on a light from the house. She's wearing *my* ring. My hand catches hers and studies it.

"What a beautiful ring." I force my smile.

She gives Dante a look before replying, "Thank you. It means the world to me."

I swallow the saliva pooling in my mouth. My body heats and I can't look at Dante.

I drop her hand. "Excuse me." This is too much. I'm in over my head.

My fake smile drops the moment I turn. I must look rude and crazy right now. I don't know why I thought Dante would keep that ring, why I always assumed I'd be the one wearing it. It makes no rational sense.

I walk to the edge of the property, thankful for the shadows that shield my movements from prying eyes. My chest heaves with each ragged breath I take in time with my thundering pulse. I'm out of my element here. All I want to do is curl up in Oakleigh's bed and cuddle her. She's always been my anchor, the reason I have kept going.

I wrap my arms around my middle, fighting back my sad thoughts. I hate that I couldn't have done more; for myself, for my daughter, for Dante and our past.

Nausea squeezes my stomach, twisting it so hard it's almost unbearable.

My hand goes into my pocket and I quickly unwrap a candy. Its sweet flavor only cramps my insides more instead of relieving the pressure. I unwrap another, hoping this one will ease my pain. My tummy revolts with each step I take, forcing me to place two fingers into my mouth and throw up everything I've eaten today.

In moments like this, my sensitive stomach always makes an appearance. The overwhelming sensation builds until I can't take it anymore, and I fix the pain by emptying my stomach. It's the only control I have over it. I feel suffocated and I hate myself for doing it.

Using my palm, I wipe my mouth and look for a place to sit but there's nothing to comfortably lean against or sit on. I plant myself down in the shadows and lie on the soft, lush grass. The night stars are clouded over, leaving a black sky with only the party lights illuminating the area.

"I never thought I'd see the day when Demi Gallo looked jealous."

My head lolls to the side to find a cocky-looking Dante, before I look back to the starless sky. He stands over me, blocking my view. Why must he look gorgeous and happy while I'm having an internal meltdown?

He surprises me by sitting down next to me.

"The grass might stain your expensive suit."

He chuckles, moving around to get more comfortable.

"I thought you liked to reign over your peasants from the deck," I say, refusing to look at him. His warm hand covers mine but I don't feel his eyes on me, he must be looking at the sky. This was our favorite thing to do back in the day.

"You said no to the ring when you never showed up." His voice is soft, and his fingers rub over mine. I don't want to be having this conversation, my instincts are to avoid it at all costs. My insides tighten with the impeding conflict. I just want everyone to be happy, even if it's at the expense of my own happiness.

"That was a long time ago." I sigh.

"Savio and Charlotte got married spontaneously. He didn't have a ring. They were in the middle of their vows when I ran out of the room and gave it to them. That ring was meant for someone special. I was never going to be giving it to anyone but you, but I had to move on, and the only way I could was by letting go of that ring."

"It's not that I didn't love you, you know?" Tears try to push their way into my eyes. I blink, forcing them back as much as I can. "I was dealing with a lot back then." *And pregnant with your baby.* That same stomach-twisting crunch grasps hold of my middle when I think back to that day. "I had planned to come back to you." I should have never left his roof to pack a bag and just left with the clothes on my back. It was a silly idea to want to bring Stitches with us. All of the what ifs I've thought about every day since then cross my mind.

A tear leaks from the side of my eyes. *I'm stronger than this, stop being a child.*

"I just don't understand. Was it you wanted more? Was I not good enough?" The vulnerability that laces his tone has my guilt sitting heavy on my chest.

I stay silent, not knowing how to respond and scared my voice will break the moment I try to speak.

"The thing is, you always come back. I hate being the butt of a joke." His gaze is looking past me, as if he's not here in the moment, but somewhere else.

Dante was my whole world. I tried to show that the only way I knew how but, never having positive role models, I often questioned how I should act.

"It was never you," I whisper, my voice cracking at the end.

Dante scoffs, removing his hand from on top of mine. "It's me, not you." He mimics my voice in a horrible rendition. "It's stuff like this that I'm talking about. You could never let me in. You let me fix your problems, but never trusted me enough for anything that mattered."

"It's never been like that. You are the *one* person I trust in the whole world."

"Do you hear yourself?" he balks. "Do you *actually* believe that or are you still trying to convince yourself of it?"

He stands and I quickly sit up. I hate when we fight and I don't know how to fix it. The truth would make it all that much more difficult. He would hate me and I don't think I could survive knowing he despises me.

"You can move in with the other girls tomorrow."

My heart cracks and I wipe more tears from my eyes. *This is a good thing.* I need to distance myself from Dante, otherwise the truth will come pouring out of me. What's the point of hurting us both more than we have already done? *This is a good thing.* Hopefully, it will help the girls finally accept me. I could use a friend. I have no one, and it's my fault.

My hands push against the ground to help me stand. It takes a second to calm my racing heart and try to get my head in check. My nose flares as I take a deep breath before I push one foot in front of the other to join the party once again.

Dante stays rooted in place, and that familiar searing sensation burns my back. It has the small hairs on my neck feeling electrified. The sensation stays until I reach the crowd, and by then I can't help myself. I glance over my shoulder to where I left him but he's no longer there.

Chapter 16

Dante

I STAND AT THE back of the warehouse as my brother, Max, dismantles a guy one piece at a time while keeping him alive. I fucking hate this part of the job. "He obviously knows nothing. Can we kill him and get on with our day?" I ask.

"Why is he in a mood?" Max asks my other brothers.

"He's not getting laid," Romeo teases.

"Demi is moving in with the girls today," Savio adds.

"And what's the history with this girl?" Max asks.

"She's no one," I reply with a sneer.

"She used to live across the street from us when we lived with Ma," Savio informs everyone.

Our guest of honor moans and I can't take it anymore. I walk up beside Max and put a bullet in his head.

"I thought you were a lover, not a fighter." Max bumps my shoulder, frowning at the now-dead body hunched over itself.

"He was our only lead, dipshit," Savio curses.

"Naw, the guy knew nothing. He would have talked if he had," Max says, picking up a rag to wipe his hands.

Savio places a hand over his forehead, frustrated. He would never hesitate to kill anyone if he thought they posed a danger to his wife. He's gone along with her conspiracy theories that someone among our ranks tried to help get her killed.

I don't know if I agree. This is all over some random computer IP address, but I keep my mouth shut. If I had a wife, I would want to shield her from everything as well, no matter the cost.

Max hits me on the back of the shoulder. "I need you to head out with me today."

I don't want to return to my empty home and I have no interest in seeing Demi at my club, so I agree. "You got it."

Max pulls up to my strip club and my fingers dig into my thigh. "For a guy who says he can find his own date, you seem to be coming in here an awful lot."

He turns to me. "Here's the thing. I've been digging deeper. Somehow, our bank accounts are being skimmed. It's small, a few cents a day, but over many accounts it's adding up. I think I've found a lead and the IP address is the same one Savio is looking for. It has to be linked."

"That doesn't address why we're here." I dread walking into my own club. How pathetic is this? And it's because of some girl.

"It's coming from a computer in *your* club."

My mouth opens. "Since when do you know anything about finance or computers?"

"Simmer the fuck down. I'm not accusing you of anything."

"I should have known to be on alert when The Butcher asked to take a drive."

"I'm acting as your brother. I have no ulterior motives, I promise."

"Romeo had you come into town because of this, not because Savio wanted you at his wife's birthday party. I should have seen it," I scoff.

"Listen, *he* noticed the skimming and I looked into it. He doesn't even know I found a lead. I'm bringing it up to you first but he's going to have to learn the truth soon."

I stare out at the cheap-looking neon sign on the top of the building that shines Throne of Sin. I've been wonderful to all these girls. Without me, I doubt many would have survived past a few years. They would have been found as Jane Does in ditches. None of them have families or anyone who has the energy or resources to look for them. I've stuck my reputation on the line for them. Everyone thinks your life is over once I own you. It's how I've ensured their safety and well-being.

My mind races through what I know of each girl as I try to work out which of them would backstab me.

"No one is blaming you, Dante."

"It's the fucking principal of it all." I curl my fingers in; they're tight and stiff. Violence has never been my first reaction. "Let's go in."

I slam the car door behind me.

"I knew I shouldn't have told you," Max says under his breath. When I look behind me, he's shaking his head like I'm the one acting like an idiot.

I use my foot to kick the long horizontal bar on the door to open it. The bouncer schools his questioning look and stands when he sees that it's me.

"Hi, Boss."

I don't answer and keep walking. Behind me, I hear Max introducing himself like they could be best friends. I don't need my entire family with their fingers in my business. I can handle this myself.

A few of the girls see me and immediately turn around and pick up their pace with serving drinks. My face must say it all right now. I do a lap around, scrutinizing how everyone has acted around me in the last six months. Not a single one of them has been off.

"Need a drink, Boss Man?" Robin is the one brave enough to approach me. Even Sienna has busied herself cleaning the already-clean counter.

I look at my watch. "Where's Demi?" Her shift started two minutes ago. My eyes bounce back and forth between Robin and Sienna.

"Her and Tanya traded shifts. She would have been rushed if she started now, because of the move and all," Robin answers, looking sheepish, like she's the one in trouble.

I stay silent. *Rushed?* Everything of hers would have fit into one bag. What the hell did she have to do to settle in? It took me all of five seconds to move her into my room and all I said was, "This is your room now."

Maybe it was three seconds.

Robin stays at my side, presumably waiting for my response to her question. "I don't want a drink, Robin." Her smile brightens when I say her name.

Tanya takes Robin's spot and I struggle to control my anger. "I'm about to go into room two if you need to blow off some steam." She smiles, ducking away to get the key from Sienna.

My cheeks puff out as I blow a breath out. I make my way over to where Max is flirting with Sienna and tug at his shirt to make him follow me back to my office. When out of view, he hits my hand a bunch of times until I let go of his shirt. He closes the door and takes a seat in my big leather chair.

"What do you need from me to figure this out?" I grit out, hating that this is a thing now.

"Nothing yet, other than you continuing to welcome me in here and allowing me to talk to your girls."

I raise a brow. "*Just* talking?"

He grins. "I'll be spending time with each of them at some point. Just keep your panties out of a knot and we'll be fine."

My eyes widen and he holds up his hands, laughing. "You are way too serious. You need to relax. When was the last time you took a break?"

I glare at him. "We can't all live in the middle of nowhere."

"I get my work done the same as you." He crosses his arms, looking perfectly at ease.

"Fine." What else is there to say or do?

Chapter 17

Demi

It's been a week since I moved and I haven't seen hide nor hair of Dante. I don't know why I expected him to check in on me to see how I'm doing. He's even been conspicuously absent from work, replaced by his brother Max.

I hope this has nothing to do with me.

The thought is so absurd I roll my eyes and focus back on work. I don't have that type of power over Dante.

Tonight, I'm waitressing in my black corset and booty shirts.

"Hey, Demi." Max gives me a smile. He's been flirting with all the girls. He might *seem* friendly, but I know when someone is trying to gain something. I don't trust him. His presence puts me on edge.

"Dante!" Sienna calls out. My back stiffens, suddenly nervous.

I can smell Dante before I see him. He places a firm hand on mine and his brother's shoulder as he positions himself between the two of us. My skin lights with warmth from his touch. I turn my head to acknowledge his presence.

"How's the new place?" he asks, his hand still resting on my shoulder.

"Um, ah." It takes a second for my tongue to work properly. "Tanya is my roommate. Her and Robin drew straws."

"I noticed you've been avoiding certain shifts, and she's picked them up for you."

I repeat his words, not understanding them. "I work the shifts Sienna scheduled me for." Tanya needed me to trade some shifts with her for personal reasons, and I'm not going to throw her under the bus. She's finally accepting me, even though she's the only girl in the house having to share a room.

"Next time you want to switch a shift, it needs to go through me first." His hand leaves my shoulder.

"I don't see the other girls going to you to approve changes. So, I'll continue doing as them, by taking up any shift changes with your manager, Sienna." I hold his glare refusing to back down.

"Careful with that tongue of yours, Demi." I watch as he works the back of his jaw over and back.

"If all of us girls are going to be going to you for shift changes, you should inform Sienna before any of us. It's called manners."

Dante's eyes flare with my back talk.

"Hey Demi, you want to hang out on your day off?" Max asks pushing himself between the two of us.

"I can't." I gather up my drinks onto my tray and leave to do my job.

I can feel eyes on me the entire time. When I sneak a look back at the bar, both brothers are staring. It's unnerving. I don't want to go back to the bar, but I have no choice.

When I return, Max strikes up a conversation. "Why can't you hang out?" His posture is relaxed except for a small tick in his left eye. If I had a vision of what a mafia man looked like, it would be Max.

"The girls and I are hanging out." I grab my drinks, turning my back to him, not wanting to talk about this anymore.

For the rest of my shift, I talk to the customers more than normal, avoiding spending any time near Max. People surround the bar three bodies deep, making avoidance easy enough. The room has become overcrowded and I have to push through people to get Sienna my list of drinks.

My ass gets grabbed at least twice while I try to take my drinks away from the bar, but I'm too busy to see who is responsible. The girls on stage are getting cat called and the bouncer has already had to step in because of coins being shot toward the girls.

I'm happy I'm not on stage tonight. I'm working triple time on the floor because all of our lap dance girls are in the rooms, even the small curtained areas are in use, and it's leaving less of us on the floor to deliver drinks. This weekend has been far crazier than our normal.

After delivering the most recent round of drinks, I turn to head back to the bar and collide with a hard chest, my round tray falling to the ground with a clatter.

"You must be new around here." The man picks up my tray and holds it out to me, but his fingers stay gripping its edge as I try to take it back.

"Yeah, sorry. Thanks." I pick up an empty beer bottle from the table next to us and try to tug the tray from his grasp. He doesn't let go.

"What's your name?"

Before I can reply, a regular has moved between us. "Leave Demi alone. She's off limits."

"This is between her and me." The stranger tries to push the regular out of the way and I take a few steps back, only to be stopped by the gathering crowd.

"No, you don't understand. She's Dante's."

The stranger turns his back, ignoring the warning. Out of the corner of my eye, I watch as the regular cracks his bottle over the table, shattering glass. My tray is dropped to the ground as the men square off at each other. The regular lunges at the stranger with his jagged bottle and I'm pushed forward by the throng of bodies crammed into the room. I don't know what to do. On instinct, I break the bottle I'm holding, in case I need to use it.

My heart is pounding out of my chest and my fingers grip the neck tighter.

The stranger flicks open his curved pocket knife, swiping at the face of his opponent. I try to step around, but bodies bump into me, pushing me into the fight. I arch my back, missing the glass bottle that swoops near my face, before it's poked into the stranger's arm and pulled back out a moment later. A few droplets of blood sprinkle across my chest. I have no time to react before my head is whipped back from the force of my hair being pulled.

"I bet you're a great fuck."

Automatically, my hand pushes down into the side of his leg with my broken glass bottle, and I'm able to turn to face the man. His face is red, his lips snarling. I watch as he tries to reach into his jacket, but is lunged at before he's able to grab anything. I bet he has a gun.

The loud music is cut, but the room is just as loud with it off as it was with it on. Over the top of the crowd I see men shoving their way forward, but I'm scared they won't make it here in time.

Six big looking men storm over, pushing me out of the way to get to the fighting men.

My hand lands on a bunch of small pieces of glass. My palm by the thumb has a large piece of glass sticking out of it. I watch as blood runs over my hand, landing on the floor. It doesn't even hurt. I'm bumped around some more, while I stand in place, picking glass out of my skin. It's impossible to move far. As soon as I pull out the sizable chunk, blood pours out of my hand like a river.

I stumble, my head feeling light, and have to place my hand on a table to steady myself.

"Ah shit, Dem." I look up to find Dante staring down at my hand. He places his own over mine, pulling me out of the crowd and toward his office.

"I'm fine. I just need a Band-Aid."

"What you *need* is stitches." He opens the door, grabbing a shirt to wrap around my hand. Crimson seeps through the fabric within seconds.

"Keep pressure on it." He uses his own hand to show me the amount of pressure needed before he lets go and rounds his desk.

He pulls a first aid kit from one of his drawers, dumping all of its contents onto the desk and gathers what he needs.

My light-headedness is making it hard to stand up, so I wobble to the leather seat across from his and fall into it. Pain begins to work through the euphoric haze of adrenaline as I take a deep breath to make the dizziness go away.

I try to ignore the pain, but it's hopeless. Dante pulls over a stool and sits in front of me. He takes my hand in his and gently removes the wrapping. I turn my head because the look of the gash is making my stomach swish with nausea.

"You never do anything halfway, huh? It always has to be a hundred percent or nothing. This is going to take at least ten stitches."

"What can I say? I'm an overachiever."

"Where was our ambition when we were in school? Might've actually helped back then"

"Speak for yourself; I graduated with honors," I reply with pride.

His hand pauses from cleaning my wound. "I didn't know that."

"That's because I never mentioned it. People look at me differently when they find out I'm smart. It's like I lose all of my street credit and, for most of my life, street cred has been a matter of survival."

He takes my hand and places it over the gauze he'd been using to clean the wound, while he pulls out a needle and what looks like string.

"Have you ever stitched anyone up before?"

He gives me that panty-dropping boyish smirk I used to love so much. "I have a jar of bullets that I've pulled out of Savio. I stitch him up all the time. I'm a pro, you won't even have a scar."

"Have you ever been shot?" I ask.

He looks up from threading his needle and his eyes hold mine. "Why? You worried about me?"

The pain in my palm thunders to the staccato beat of my pulse. The air crackles with electricity that coils around us. "I'm always worried about you. You never strayed far from my mind." I swallow the lump in my throat.

Dante clears his throat and loops my first stitch.

"I came back, you know," I mention quietly. I hate that he thinks I never cared enough to return.

His eyes connect with mine once again and pain radiates through his dark irises. Dante is the one person I never wanted to hurt.

"But you and Savio were already gone." I remember all the awful things his mother yelled at me when I knocked on her door. She thought I was the reason her sons left her.

My hand shakes in his but he doesn't comment on it.

"All you had to do was tell me to wait, Demi." He refocuses on my stitches. The air is almost too thick to breathe in.

"I never planned to make you wait. If I could go back in time, I would have never left your roof that night." A decade of emotions crash into my heart. This is my biggest regret in life. I open my mouth to try to tell him what happened that night, but I've never spoken about it to anyone. I can't get the words up no matter how hard I try.

"But you did. And I didn't hear from you for a decade." His voice is laced with hurt and I hate that I caused it.

Why do I have to be so defective? He would understand instantly, but the trauma is too thick and I can't bring myself to spit it out. Instead, I cop out and say, "I had no idea where you went. When

I walked in here for the first time, I didn't even know you owned this place." Tears fight their way into my eyes.

He finishes with my hand and places a soft kiss over his work. It sends a shiver down my spine.

"I'm sorry, Dante. I wish I could say more."

"We've always been on different pages and you've never trusted me enough to let me in fully. Right now is no different."

The truth is painful to hear. "I trust you more than anyone else in my life," I whisper, my voice thick with clogged sadness.

"I think that's what hurts me the most." He stands up and I worry he's going to leave me alone. Instead, he opens up a small mini fridge and takes out an ice pack, placing it in my hand.

My entire body trembles and I hate how foolish I feel for not being able to stay still. I wish I had some type of comeback for Dante, something that would make him feel better and give him a reason to look at me like he used to.

I need him to hold me like he once did. It always fixed everything in the moment.

"Lift your hands." He fixes his oversized sweater on me.

"Why do you have these old clothes when all you ever wear are suits now?"

"It helps to remind me of my roots."

He holds my hand, his eyes lowering to my lips. I want him to kiss me, even though he shouldn't. I'm afraid he's going to see my rapid heartbeat pounding through his sweater. My body naturally moves closer a millimeter at a time. Dew beads across my skin as I heat. Dante mimics my position and the air zips around us, ready to ignite at the first spark.

In slow motion, my lips touch his. They press against each other, relieving the stress building in me. His tongue sweeps across my lips and I open for him. His hand slips to my neck, wrapping behind to keep me in place. The sensation of his thumb circling my pounding pulse and the way his lips devour mine has my head floating in the clouds. I moan with pleasure. I forgot how exceptional of a kisser Dante is.

I would do anything he asked if he kept kissing me like this. My unharmed hand steadies me by pressing down on his thigh.

A knock on the door has Dante pulling away from me and his stool falls when he's forced to stand. Clearing his throat, he goes to open the door. Robin is standing there, shifting from foot to foot, looking nervous. The room's energy changes and I hear Robin say, "We just wanted to make sure Demi was alright and see if she needed to go to the hospital."

"She's fine. I just finished stitching her up. One of you will have to take her home." My heart sinks at how stiff and uncaring he sounds. "I can't have her serving drinks and bleeding on the customers."

I stand, unable to force a smile.

"Nice shirt," Robin comments.

"Dante got it in the lost and found."

Dante's eyes turn dark when they narrow on me, but I don't care. I'm mad at how he's making me feel.

"I think I might actually keep it."

Chapter 18

Dante

"Don't you find it weird that you haven't seen Demi in ten years, and then *bam*, she's working off a debt to you?" Max scratches at his jaw. "And she's the only girl who hasn't jumped at the chance to spend time with me." His expression is to say that no woman has ever turned him down before. "She's skittish around me and almost everyone." It's comical how stumped Max is by her. It makes me proud that she has shown no interest in him. My brother isn't exactly a slouch in the looks department.

"Give her some credit. That girl can sense a serial killer when she sees one. Anyway, she's fine around me." I lean back in my chair and take a sip of my drink, trying to cover my cocky grin.

"I'm not a serial killer," he scoffs, annoyed that I turned the conversation back on him. "What if she planned this whole thing and came in here pretending she didn't know it was your place? What if she knew about you buying women and decided to try her luck?"

The thought puts a bad taste in my mouth and I set my drink down. "That's one elaborate plan to get my attention. I don't see her doing that for a second."

"She's hiding something. I have a knack for knowing these things."

"She's not hiding anything," I argue, maintaining my relaxed posture while Max stands to pace around. This guy's mind never stops. When he thinks he smells a trail, he goes OCD on it. He's obsessive when something consumes him.

"What has she been doing for the last ten years?"

I open my mouth to say and realize I have no clue. I've been so focused on her leaving and never coming back, it never occurred to me to ask.

Max laughs at my blank expression. "You've been thinking with the wrong head, brother." He points at me, shaking his head.

"What do you suggest?"

"It's her day off tomorrow, right?"

"So?"

"You need to watch and see what she does."

Demi has been living with the girls for three weeks now. I don't normally show up where they live, but it's not like I haven't done it before. Before I knock, Robin answers the door in what looks like only a hoodie. I instantly recognize it as mine. A flash of anger zips down my spine and I have to bite my tongue to keep from asking if Demi had given her permission.

"Who knew one lost and found sweater would be so popular?" I say, stepping inside. I don't need permission to enter a house I pay for.

"Demi tossed it in the garbage." She shrugs. "Finders, keepers."

My back molars grind.

It doesn't take long for the girls to come out of their rooms once they hear my voice.

"Why, Mr. Mancini, it's a pleasure to have you over," Tanya purrs.

I look around and notice Demi isn't around. "Where's Demi?"

A few of the girls look put out, but Tanya looks all too happy to answer. "She never hangs out with us on days off unless you're there. Even some nights she doesn't come home right away."

That's all news to me. I hate that Max might have been on to something.

"And where does she go?" I try to keep my voice pleasant, but the girls shift, looking more worried with my tone.

I look around the room and my eyes land on Robin. The two of them seem to be friends. "Well, shit," she drawls, and narrows her eyes on Tanya. "She goes to the inner city."

Fucking prescription drugs. "Why?"

Robin shakes her head. "I ain't no snitch, but I honestly don't know. The less I'm involved, the better."

She doesn't seem to be lying. I nod in response. "Know where in the inner city?"

"I think I do," Tanya answers. "I could go show you." The last thing I want is to be alone with these women. I normally have Sienna with me for shit like this.

All I have to do is ask around a few times and I find Demi. She has a line of women waiting for her. I was expecting her to be trying to find a dealer. Maybe so high she forgot where she was. Or maybe a client had somehow convinced her to meet him somewhere. But this...I scratch my head, confused. I have no idea what this is.

I step out of my car and pass the line, heading for Demi. She's too busy to spot me coming right for her. She hands a woman a jar of what looks like pills. *Is she dealing now?*

I look more closely at the line, needing time before I lose my cool. Half of these women are teens, maybe slightly older. Suddenly, their protruding bellies become apparent. It's a line of pregnant teens. My brother, the Mancini Don, is going to lose his shit if what I think is occurring, actually is.

"Demi Gallo, fancy seeing you here."

She startles at my voice. "Dante." Her cheeks flush while she places both hands in the pockets at the back of her jeans.

"What are you doing?" I ask, not able to keep my angry tone down.

"You need to relax." She places her hands on my chest.

My eyes widen and my nose flares at being told what to do.

"Alright girls, I have to cut it short today. See you next week." There are groans from all around before the line disperses, leaving us alone.

I refuse to be the one who speaks first.

"How did you know where I was?" she asks with her hand on her jetted out hip.

"I know everything about my club including where my girls are."

"I suppose this is when you're going to tell me that if I leave the house I need to let you know where I'm going."

"Something like that." My tongue slides over the top of my teeth.

"Follow me." Demi takes my hand and leads me around the block. "Did you know this area has an overwhelming rate of teenage pregnancy? A lot of parents in this area can hardly feed themselves. You remember how it was in my house after my dad disappeared."

I scoff, "Yeah, you no longer walked down the street with a black eye."

"It's easy for you to say when you weren't the one living it. Hell, you left shortly after." Demi holds up her finger when I open my mouth to interrupt. "You have no idea what struggles I had, and don't even try to pretend that you know."

"For a brilliant girl like yourself, I can't understand how you don't know that you were one beating away from being murdered."

"Don't stand here all high and mighty on me. My father's beatings hurt less than the stomach cramps and knowing I was worth only as much as my body." A sarcastic, disbelieving chuckle escapes her pouty lips. "Anyway, the beatings didn't stop because he left."

I straighten, not understanding. "What the fuck do you mean?"

"He had debts, Dante." A tear escapes the corner of her eye. "They had to be paid by someone."

My body tremors with a new rage building in me. I've never been overly emotional, but Demi has a way of bringing it out of me.

"What are you talking about?" I swallow thickly, my body covered with goosebumps.

"I didn't meet you that night because I landed myself in the hospital. His bookie needed to send a message and he couldn't find my mom. My beating was the message."

My hand tightens around hers and another tear escapes as she tries to wipe it away. She turns her head to stop looking at me.

"Don't hide your pain from me." I deserve to see it. I would have paid the debt off, if I had known. It guts me, my stomach turning to stone. "Tell me what happened." It's impossible to keep my voice even.

"I can't..." She takes a shuddering breath and I can see how hard it is for her to talk. "I refuse to be dragged down by the past. It has taken me a long time to get it in check and won't allow it to be my undoing. I can't go back to that dark place." Her voice breaks and I step in to hold her. My arms wrap around her body and her face is pushed against my chest.

"I'm so sorry." The apology is worthless, it will never change the past or ease her hurt and suffering. I listen to the sound of her trying to get her breathing under control.

She has such a tight grip on my heart that mine squeezes as if it were hers.

I don't have to ask who the bookie is. There was only one back then, and he won't be alive much longer if he hasn't already gotten himself killed.

"Tell me about what you're doing here?"

She lifts her head from my chest. "The feeling of being a poor girl in a poverty-stricken town is something I remember and I want to help. I give the girls prenatal vitamins because they can't afford them. A while back, I worked with a midwife for a number of years. I try to give advice to the girls when I can. These girls have no health care and are scared. I just hope to make the transition a little easier on them."

Now I feel like an ass for thinking the worst of her.

"You're the kindest person I know." *Literally.* "I think this is a great thing."

She lays her head back down on my chest, hugging me back.

"Can I take you for a cup of coffee?" I ask seriously.

She laughs into my chest, the vibrations going straight to my heart, and I sigh. It just feels right to have her in my arms, and right now, it's like no time has passed. We're still two teenagers sitting on a roof talking about life.

Chapter 19

Demi

"You're getting cut early tonight, Demi," Sienna calls from behind the bar.

"Really?" I go to check the time, but there isn't a clock around to remind anyone of time commitments. "What time is it?" It doesn't feel late.

"Late enough." I've worked slower nights and never gotten off early. All of us girls all leave at the same time.

"Okay..." I draw out the word, confused. "Did I do something wrong?"

Sienna rolls her eyes. "This is a gift, just take it."

I nod, still not understanding, but go to the dressing room to change into my street clothes. I don't even have a cell phone or watch to check the time. Oh well, it will give me more time downtown.

"Where are you headed?" Robin asks when she sees me walking out in street clothes.

"I was told they don't need me on the floor for tonight."

Robin glances over at Sienna and replies under her breath, "She's probably just angry you're killing it in tips."

As I walk out of Throne of Sin, I'm forced to protect my eyes from the light glaring into them. The sun is low on the horizon, its angle hitting me perfectly, stunning me with a beautiful pink and orange sunset. I turn to head toward the bus station and find Dante leaning against his car.

"Need a ride?" he asks with a cocky smile.

Giddiness swarms through me. "I'm not headed home," I reply.

"I know. Remember, I said I'd go with you next time." *He remembered.* The gesture is small but makes my heart constrict.

He walks around his car and opens the door for me as he waits. Hesitantly, I walk toward him.

"Thank you, sir," I say, sliding up to him.

He stares at me, and my hand fiddles with my hair unsure what he's looking at. "Fuck, I forgot how beautiful your smile was."

A slow blush creeps up my neck as I slip into his passenger seat and he closes the door behind me. He moves around to his side and leaves me with my heart pounding in my chest.

Dante stands a foot behind like a wall of steel, ready to stop anything that may cause me harm. It's adorable, but is also scaring everyone away.

I turn to him and place a kiss on his smooth jaw, then freeze, realizing my action. It's just been so comfortable around Dante, like we're back to who we used to be with each other. My cheeks flush and I say, "You need to sit, or lean against a wall. Do something to make yourself look less intimidating. None of these women will come around with you looking all sniper like."

His one eyebrow rises above his shades and he grunts, but he takes off his sunglasses, placing them in the open collar of his dress shirt.

"Maybe take the suit jacket off?" I suggest.

He shrugs off the jacket but, in doing so, reveals the four guns strapped around his waist and chest. It's impossible to fight my smile.

"Put the jacket back on." I shake my head, loving the ease of our conversation. "You don't even have enough hands for the number of guns you're carrying. Why four?"

"When the first two run out of ammo, I'll have backups."

"Listen, I love that you are here, but you have to go." His brows shoot up into his hairline. "I mean this in the nicest possible way. These women are scared of men like you." I run a hand through my hair. "Any man being here is just too much. Would you mind staying in your car, far far away? Please."

I wait for the explosion that's bound to happen. My muscles tighten in anticipation.

"I can't protect you from my car," he says matter of factly.

"Who are you protecting me from? Think about it. You saw the line up last time. It's a bunch of pregnant ladies worried they don't have what it takes to make it in this world as a mom. Trust me, I can handle myself."

"My car, huh?" he repeats. I grab hold of his hand and lead him into the street toward his car. "You're serious?"

"I've been doing this on my own for years. Maybe not this city, but in other places. Want to know a fun fact?"

We stop in front of his car.

"I know what I'm doing, and can hold my own. I've delivered fifteen babies, out on the streets, and not once have I had security."

He looks to be thinking about what I said. "With the midwife you worked with?"

"No." I shake my head. "Myself. The first baby I delivered was on a sidewalk just like this. It gave me the greatest feeling. My adrenaline was high and I felt like I was doing something worthwhile with my life. I loved that feeling. That's why I started to help with teen pregnancies in poverty-stricken areas. Soon, word got around and it was no longer just teens searching me out. I don't have a piece of paper saying I'm a midwife, but I read all of their textbooks and have the experience of working with one. For a lot of these women, the only options they have are to either go it alone or come to me."

"That's impressive." Dante keeps glancing at the two women loitering by a lamppost. "Recognize those two?"

"Yeah, they'll come over the moment you disappear. Trust me on this."

"Fuck. For the record I hate this. But, I won't ruin it for you. You know where I am when you finish."

"Thank you," I give him a peck on the cheek. "I don't mind if you drive further down the street or maybe down the block."

Dante

"I don't mind if you drive further down the street or maybe down the block." Demi smiles, batting her long thick lashes. I take a look around the area. I hate that I'm caving, but it's obvious she's made it this far without me.

"You won't even know I'm here. I promise."

I slip into my car, and turn on the engine. The moment my wheels begin to roll, the two women on the sidewalk move to stroll up to her.

It takes no time to find an inconspicuous place to park and pull out my binoculars.

I watch in awe as Demi takes the time to help each lady who appears in the parking lot. Her full attention always remains on the woman in front of her. She gives advice, takes measurements, and hands out prenatal vitamins. She's obviously at a disadvantage because she has no medical equipment or private room, but that doesn't seem to bother anyone.

This is the first time I have truly seen Demi happy, without worry, and it's a sight to behold. Could she have been telling the truth about not doing drugs? But then, who the hell had she been sneaking off to call? I take out my phone and send Max a message asking him to find out.

It's not even five minutes later I get a notification from my brother. I look up at Demi, watching her do her thing and avoiding the report I need to read. She must be able to feel my eyes on her, because she looks up her emerald eyes searching for my whereabouts. My heart constricts, and I lean back in my seat, resting the binoculars on the passenger side.

I immediately recognize the name to whom the number belongs. Her mother. As I continue reading, I realize it's her who's addicted to prescription drugs. I didn't realize she was close enough to her mother to lie about something like that. She used to tell me everything.

My phone buzzes with a message from Max. **She's clouding your judgment, brother. This call wasn't all that long ago.**

Me: **Stop being a drama queen.**

Max: **You can't change people. History always has a way of repeating itself.**

I refuse to respond. I know Demi better than anyone.

Chapter 20

Dante

GOOSEBUMPS PRICKLE OVER MY skin from under my suit as my brothers and I stalk our prey. We're back in Savio's and my old stomping grounds and the area immediately puts me in a bad mood. I hated everything about this Hell hole back then, and by the looks of it, it's only gotten worse over the last decade.

"Look at you, wanting to get your hands dirty. I never thought I'd see the day." Max jumps around, way too happy for my liking.

Savio laughs at the spectacle he's making of himself before mocking me. "What happened to your *"I'm a lover, not a fighter"* attitude?"

I should have done this without asking for help. The moment I called Savio, he instantly went to Max, since he's the expert, and here the three of us are now.

Changing the subject I ask, "By chance do any of you know what equipment a prenatal clinic would need?" Both my brothers side eye me.

"You got a pregnancy kink? Can't say I've tried that one out myself." Max's face is serious and he stares off with a smirk on his face. "I think I would dig it."

"How pregnant does the chick have to be? Two months? Four months?" Savio adds.

I flip the bird to both my brothers who are now laughing at my expense.

"Nine months!" Savio exclaims. Looks like I'm going to have to do the research myself.

We grow silent, when the bookie appears walking into a run-down pub. We've already cased the place and know about his office in the basement. I can't believe this fucker is still alive.

"What did he do?" Max asks.

My tongue swipes over my front teeth. "He hurt what's mine."

"You're still on the Demi band wagon, huh?" He slants me a disapproving look that I want to punch off his face. "I get it, she's a hot piece of ass."

My composure breaks and my fist flies out, hitting him square in the nose. Blood pours like a faucet, spilling over his suit. "I'm tired of you speaking poorly of her. Shut your mouth from now on."

"What the hell, man?" He pinches the bridge of his nose, but the front of his shirt is covered already.

I push my hand through my hair.

"How do you expect me to save the fun stuff for you when you get me amped up like this?" Max teases, not fazed by my outburst. Romeo would have kicked my ass.

We stand by Savio's car, waiting for the man of the hour to reemerge.

When he finally does, several hours later, we follow him through the dark streets to a decrepit house.

"Go grab him, Dante."

I look behind me to Max. "You said you like the chase," I counter.

"I'm covered in dried blood. He'll take one look at me and run."

Savio snickers.

"Shut up or I'll put another bullet in you," I tease.

"You're just jealous that I've survived multiple gunshot wounds, and that makes me tougher than you," Savio brags, lifting his shirt up to show off the scars he wears proudly.

"You're both assholes." I slip out of the car with a small metal bat in my hands. The house has no door. I move a large piece of wood to the side and slip in, just like our man did.

"Ahhhhhhhhh!" The bookie runs toward me with a Swiss Army knife. I step to the side, swinging the bat before he turns around. The metal connects, flattening him to the ground with zero fight. I expected this to go down differently. I walk around him, nudging him with my foot. Not a muscle moves. He's going to be a heavy bastard to carry out of here. I pick him up under his arms and drag him to our car. My brothers watch with amusement as they make me do all the work before we head toward our warehouse.

For the first time in my life, I don't hate entering the old, smelly building. I tie our guy's feet to the chair, but that's it. I want him to think he has a chance.

Savio dumps a pail of cold water over his head and the bookie slowly stirs. His hand goes to where I hit him and a smile breaks across my face.

"Why, hello." My voice has him freezing and his eyes dart to the three of us. He tries to stand, but with his legs tied, he only manages to fall forward. I take pleasure in watching him squirm and try to get his feet free.

"Sit in the chair," I command, my voice so harsh I don't even recognize it as my own.

He just looks at me like I'm stupid, so I step forward, sliding my brass knuckles on for him to see. He still doesn't move. I sucker punch him in the stomach before tossing his body back where I want it.

"Damn, Dante. Who knew you had this in you?" Savio mumbles with pride in his tone.

I block him and Max out as they gossip like school girls behind me.

I pull out a picture of Demi from when we used to live across the street from each other. The corners are curled and it has a few creases throughout the picture, but it's the only one I have of her. I've kept it hidden in my wallet all these years…until now.

"Know this girl?" I ask, my baritone voice unwavering.

"Never seen her in my life."

I punch him again and the chair rocks back on its rear legs as he moans in pain.

"I'm asking one more time. Do you recognize this girl?"

He takes the picture out of my hands and studies it. "Yeah, I've seen her around."

"You beat her almost to death ten years ago."

"Maybe this is the time I show you the hospital report." Max says behind me. I raise my hand for him to stop.

"Demi told me enough, I don't need to read the report."

I punch the bookie again, this time in the face. A sickly crack rings out in the darkness and his hand cups his jaw.

"You beat her to send a message to her father, who was dead, by the way."

"That's not true," he mumbles, having a hard time talking.

I lift a brow, allowing him time to continue speaking.

"He didn't owe me anything, I just said that. I was paid to rough her up, and then her mother gave me the money I had lied about. It felt like a win-win at the time."

I crack my neck, one side at a time.

"I'm sorry. I didn't know she was anyone special."

Max hands me a knife.

"Please don't kill me. I have a wife and grandchildren."

"This is for hurting Demi!" The plan was to only take a few fingers, but I can't control the rage building in me. I run at him, shoving the knife through his chest. It's how my heart felt when I heard someone hurt Demi.

I'm huffing when I take a step back. A hand rests on my shoulder, offering comfort, but I turn and forcefully remove it.

"You forgot to ask who paid him, asshole," Savio reprimands.

I look over at Max, who looks like a proud father. "It feels good, doesn't it?" He smirks. "Don't worry, I'll look into it for you." He shrugs, uncaring I fucked up. "I've always loved a good chase."

The adrenaline pours through me. I feel fantastic and wish I could do it again.

Max pats my shoulder before stepping forward. "I'll tap myself in and deal with the body. If you ever want to come hunting with me, let me know." I know he's not talking about animals in a forest. His specialty is tracking people and taking them out. He goes to his black duffle bags and arranges an assortment of knives and saws.

I slip the brass knuckles off and place them in my pocket.

"Let's go have a beer. I think we could both use one," Savio offers, already making his way toward the exit. I hear a chain saw turn on from behind and don't bother looking back.

A beer sounds perfect right now.

Chapter 21

Demi

"Demi, Boss Man wants to talk to you about some discrepancies with your cash out," Sienna calls for all the girls to hear. I have no idea what she's talking about. I've never stolen a day in my life. The other girls give me strange looks while shaking their heads and I blow out a breath, suddenly hot and nervous. My only defense is that someone is setting me up. My first guess would be Tanya. She hates being the only one having to share a room. Me being gone would give her the space back that she so desperately craves. I still can't get a good read on her. She's hot and cold, no matter how hard I try.

I cast a glance over my shoulder at her. "Good luck!" Sienna calls, and I can't tell if she's being sarcastic or not.

My hand knocks on the closed door and Dante answers, "Come in, Miss Gallo."

Miss. Gallo, that's different.

"You wanted to see me?"

"Close the door." His tone is stern as he sits behind his desk, cocking a brow when I don't move fast enough.

Wanting to get this over with so I can go back to work, I close the door. "Good girl," he praises. "Do you want a drink?" He stands, looking handsome as ever in his tailored suit.

I shake my head no. "I'm not sure what's going on, but it's not what you think." I begin to defend myself.

"I didn't ask you to speak yet," he interrupts, his dark irises narrowing on me.

My fingers fidget with the hem of my shorts as I stand awkwardly by the closed door.

He pours two drinks and walks to the edge of his desk, placing the glasses down before he slips off his suit jacket, laying it over the back of the leather chair. He undoes his cufflinks, rolling up the sleeves of the white dress shirt underneath, showcasing his sculpted forearms.

He takes a sip of the liquid, closing his eyes, savoring the taste. When his eyes open back up, he picks up the other glass and hands it to me. "Drink," he commands.

I do as I'm told.

"Good girl."

I make a scrunched-up face as the liquid burns the whole way down my throat. His small comments shouldn't have me perking up, sitting straighter, wanting to make him proud, but they do. The air in the room changes and I'm no longer nervous. Maybe he's onto something with this drink.

"I swear, I haven't stolen any money."

He sits on the edge of his desk. "I know."

My head snaps back. "What do you mean, you know? I thought...Sienna said."

He raises his hand up for me to stop talking. "I just wanted to see you and didn't want the girls to give you a hard time over it."

"Oh." I never considered that. I look from my fingers to him. It's not lost on me he's the one with all the power as he leans above me. He'll never see me as an equal.

"I rented out a space for you to meet with your clients."

"What clients?" I ask, confused and unsure what he's trying to say.

"The pregnant women. It's too hard to do what you need on the streets, and it's not safe. Word has already been directed in that area. They should have no problem finding you."

I jump up, wrapping my arms around him. "Thank you!" I give him a kiss on the lips.

His fingers slip behind my neck and kisses me back. My body melts into him, our chests flush, both of our heartbeats colliding with each other. I never want to leave this moment between us. His hands roam down my sides and cups my ass, lifting me. I'm straddling him, my knees on the desk, him caged beneath me.

This man takes my breath away.

He shifts back, his hard length directly under me. It's impossible not to feel him grow as he pushes himself against my core.

"Dante," I pant.

"That's right, show me how grateful you are." He slaps my ass and I freeze.

I pull away, my hand cupping his jaw. His eyes are lust filled and he tries to kiss me again. "We're not going down that road again." I untangle myself from him, knowing I can't live with myself if we become what we once were. I need more. When Dante and I have sex again, it will be because we want to, not because I'm paying a debt to him. I can't do that to myself again.

"I'm not kissing you because I'm repaying a debt."

He catches my wrist, placing a kiss over my pulse. "This is who we are, Demi. It's who we always have been."

"Not anymore. My heart needs more. I need more."

He studies me seriously and I want to look away, but I keep my focus on him, watching his irises turn from a dark brown to almost black.

"Very well. You may return to work." He stands from his desk, taking a seat behind it and opening up his laptop.

Suddenly, the room feels cold and impersonal. "I'm not trying to hurt your feelings." I swallow the saliva collecting in my mouth.

He doesn't look up from his computer. "I'm glad you have placed boundaries for yourself."

It feels like a slap to my face. What I'm saying isn't coming out right. I want us to mean more.

I sigh, already seeing Dante's imaginary walls blocking anything I say. He continues to ignore me as I let myself out.

Dante

Demi closes my door and I lean back in my chair. It creaks beneath my bulk. *Demi Gallo just shot me down. Again.*

"Huh," I say out loud to the empty room. I thought she needed that from me. A smirk curls my lips. I like it when my girl gets feisty and advocates for herself.

My dick, on the other hand, is throbbing, and wants me to let it out to play. My hand palms my cock, but I remind myself I have too much to do.

I'll have to play later.

Chapter 22

Demi

"SAVIO'S FIGHTING!" I ROLL over, grabbing my alarm clock. Five o'clock! I rub my eyes to make sure I'm seeing right. I slept the whole day away.

My alarm was supposed to go off at noon so I could go into my new office for the first time. Disappointment wraps itself around me. *Shit!*

I jump out of bed and make my way out of the dark room. All the girls are up, dressed, and looking like they're about to leave.

"Looks like the princess is alive." Tanya's words are cold as she casts her eyes up and down my body before she sticks her nose in the air and turns her back to me.

"Where are you girls going?"

"Savio is having an impromptu fight. We're headed to watch."

"By that, we mean we're looking for some fresh talent to join our ranks. Last I heard, one of us is on the way out because of theft," Shelby replies, smirking at Tanya.

"Give me five minutes and I can be ready." I remember hearing about Savio's fights back in the day. I imagine he's only become more ruthless.

"We don't have time. The limo is here. Sorry," Robin answers sheepishly.

Tanya chuckles and leads the other girls out of the house, leaving Robin and me alone. "I could stay and wait for you," she offers.

I wave her off. "It's fine, I'll see you there."

"Here." She hands me a piece of paper. "It's the address."

An hour later, I hold up the piece of paper, double checking the address against that of the hole-in-the wall building in front of me. The outside looks charred from an old fire and one of the windows are boarded up, but there's a large, clean window on the other side of the steel door that shows just how busy it is inside.

I jerk the large door open and my focus is immediately pulled to the cage in the center of the space. The room is loud, buzzing with an energy that clearly has everyone excited. I head toward the back to get myself a drink, fighting through the crowded room as I make my way to the bar. It takes a while to nudge to the front of the line and I use the time to scan the crowd, looking for anyone I might recognize.

"Dante was a terror today. Did you see him?" One of the waitresses gossips behind my back. My ears immediately perk up, straining to hear.

"I keep my head down and do my work. I want no part of this conversation," a different one replies.

I finally catch sight of him out of the corner of my eye. He's by his brother, who's dressed in shorts and no shirt, his hands are taped and they're walking toward the cage.

"Savio Mancini!" The words boom through the speakers and the room erupts in applause and shouts.

"Do you think the rules don't apply to you?" The voice is close and I turn to see if they're talking to me. I frown at seeing Max.

"Excuse me?" I turn from him, my eyes following the brothers. I always envied their closeness because I've experienced nothing like it before.

"Dante's girls don't come here." My skin prickles at Max's words.

"They all said they were coming."

"They're all at Dante's, where they're *supposed* to be. I saw them with my own eyes before I headed here."

I drop my head back. Of course they would lie to me. I expected more from Robin, I thought maybe we were friends.

"Just great." First, I missed my first day at the new office and now this. I shake my head, annoyed. No matter how hard I try, it still never works out. Story of my life. "You don't have to say any more. I'm going to head to the bathroom and leave."

Weaving through the crowd, I make my way to the bathrooms. I'm fucking pissed off now. This was not how I wanted to spend my day. *What a waste!* I raise my hand to push open the bathroom door harder than necessary, but someone grabs hold of it and pulls me in the other direction.

I collide with a solid wall of muscle, the impact rattling my teeth. I'm surrounded by the familiar masculine scent I've always loved. I look up and meet Dante's hard gaze.

"Fuck off, Dante!" I'm in no mood to take his shit when I already know I messed up.

Tsk, tsk, his tongue clacks with disdain.

"I'm not in the mood right now," I reply.

He pulls me away from the bathroom and into a small side room then locks the door behind us. I'm shoved against a metal shelving unit. "I don't give a shit about your mood, Demi. You're *going* to listen to me for once in your life." His dark gaze is set firmly on me.

I wiggle to get out of his grasp, but he's too strong. His one hand brings both of my hands up, holding them against a metal bar. I try to knee him, but he moves and places himself between my legs, pinning me further. If I wasn't so pissed off, I might enjoy our little struggle.

"That office is yours, free and clear. I expect nothing from you." I stop moving, not expecting those two sentences to come from his mouth. "Today, I waited for you, and the girls showed up for you. Everyone was excited to see you succeed. I hate that you missed out on that because you didn't want to be around me. All you had to do was tell me. I would have placed one of my men there instead. I should have never been so selfish, wanting to be a part of your happiness. I suppose old habits die hard."

If I was uncertain before, I now realize, without a doubt, that I'm still in love with Dante Mancini. The feeling overwhelms me, my senses go haywire and each of my nerves feel like they're firing all at once. We're both breathing hard, our chests pushing against each other.

Needing to set the record straight, I answer, "I wanted to be there, but someone messed with my alarm clock and it never went off."

We stare at each other as he assesses if I'm telling him the truth. His eyes turn brighter and I take it as a sign he believes me.

"I wanted to be there, I swear," I whisper. "I was even looking forward to seeing you."

"I'm going to kiss you." Our chests continue to fall rapidly.

My tongue dips out and wets my lips in anticipation. The noise of the fight drifts away, leaving us in our own world. It feels like the air in the room has been sucked out and Dante has filled all the space the room had to offer.

He slants me an adoring look like he used to a decade ago. "You wanted to hangout with me, because…"

His brown eyes shine with gold specks and his other hand slips up the side of my torso.

"I missed you." I haven't been able to get Dante out of my head lately and the smile he's giving me is devastating. It causes my heart to stall.

His lips kiss me, possessive and hungry, teasing me as his tongue brushes over mine, coaxing me to open for him. The kiss is slow as we test each other. My mouth opens, our tongues twirl around each other in a seductive dance. This kiss is new. It's tender and has me hoping for things I should never wish for. This is the first real kiss we have ever shared and it is mind blowing. I've never been kissed like I'm the most important person in the world.

The world jolts back to normal speed when his hand cups my ass, and my legs wrap around his hips, locking together at the ankle. His hand slips up my shirt, pulling down the cups of my bra to feel my skin in his palm. Those perfect lips move from my mouth to my neck and I moan, feeling like I'm on cloud nine. He sucks on my collar bone, the sensation sending a shock of pleasure straight to the pit of my stomach, before he lets me down gently to free his hands, and then uses them to rip my shirt in half.

"Much better." He smirks before continuing to plaster kisses all over my skin. His fingers quickly unlatch my bra and his hands roam all over my body.

My hands thread through his hair, sliding to his shoulders, feeling the power in his muscles before they round to his back. My skirt slides up my thighs as he lifts one of my legs and wraps it around his waist. He presses closer to me, the only barrier remaining between us my panties and his pants.

"God, I've missed you," I purr with my head leaned back against the shelving unit.

"I need to feel you around my cock." He groans as my hand cups him over his pants.

"Then what are you waiting for?" My voice is husky with need and desire. I drop my leg back down and my fingers try to remove his belt, but he bats them away to do it himself. His pants fall to his knees as he lifts me once again, slides my panties to the side and enters me.

"Dante!" I cry. I forgot how big he is, how much he fills me.

He pumps into me, capturing my lips again. This kissing thing is new. He's never kissed me like this while we fucked before. He might have given me a peck, but that's it. This new side of him makes me feel cherished and protected in his arms.

My hips grind up and down, meeting each of his thrusts. "God, you feel fantastic," I pant. I look down and watch with fascination as his cock slides in and out of me.

"Tell me you want me," he demands. His face looks so vulnerable right now, even with his eyes hooded with lust.

"I've always wanted you."

He bends his head down and latches on to my nipple, sending me over the edge. I cry out with pleasure as my orgasm hits and stars shoot behind my eyes. I ride it out, grinding harder against him.

My body feels limp from the over stimulation as the end of the orgasm floats away. Dante pulls out and my legs shake as I lower myself to my knees and he releases his warm cum onto my tits.

He leans over me, cupping my jaw, and kisses me again. "Fuck, you are a sight to behold with my cum on you."

I realize, in that moment, that I hadn't even considered a condom. I know better, I'm an adult now, but something about no barrier between us has me not saying a word. We never used one before, why start now? He pulled out, we're safe. Dante doesn't look overly concerned as he uses my ripped shirt to clean me up.

"Did you want to see the place now?"

"My new office?" I grin.

"Yeah." He tosses my shirt into the trash bin.

"Don't you have a party to entertain?"

"I've hosted a hundred of them before. Savio won't even be there because he wants to spend time with his wife." He holds up his phone, typing into it, before smiling at me. "There, it's all canceled."

He kisses each breast before slipping his shirt off and onto me.

Chapter 23

Demi

I CAN'T STOP NOTICING the waitress' eyes on me as Dante leads me out of the fight club with his hand on my lower back.

"Why are your girls not allowed in there?" I ask once we're outside and no one is in earshot.

"I have a reputation to maintain. If people see them all happy and healthy and living normal lives, it would ruin my image and take away the easy lives they live." He cages me in against his car. "Why were you at the fight? Did you miss me and have to make yourself known?" he murmurs against my ear.

He thinks I was there searching him out. I could lie, tell him what he wants to hear, but that has never been us. We're honest with each other, or at least we used to be. "The girls told me they were going to the fight. I was running late because of my alarm clock and Robin gave me the address." I hold my breath, watching his expression.

It's emotionless except for the way his muscles tighten against me. "I see. Well, their error is my gain." He smiles and I let out a relieved breath.

"My thoughts exactly." I return his smile. This moment seems more intimate than it should. Like we're both in on the same secret. Electricity runs through me, sparking our chemistry once again. The parking lot disappears and we're suspended in our own bubble where the outside world no longer matters. My nipples pucker, my breath falters, and stomach flutters.

He reaches around me and opens the passenger side door. Our eyes never leave each other. To an outsider, I must look like a lovesick fool. The back of his fingers glide over my hardened nipples.

"Get in the car Demi, before I decide to fuck you for everyone to watch."

I slip in with my heart pounding. One leg bounces as fast as a telegraph machine sending Morse code, while my fingers strum against my leg. My body refuses to stay still as my excitement builds.

Dante parks his car in an out-of-the-way alleyway. The entrance to my building is off to one side, close enough to the street to be safe, yet far enough away to be discreet. The location is perfect, right in the middle of downtown.

He unlocks the four deadbolts and holds the door open for me. I step inside and wait for him to join me. He flicks on the lights and my eyes immediately prickle with tears. There's a small couch with a table and fresh flowers. I go to the flowers and lift them to my nose.

"This is beautiful," I say in awe.

He opens another room that has a bed with a roll of paper like a doctor's office.

"You'll have to come up with a name for your little spot, like a business name or symbol for people to know they're at the right place."

I walk around the small room, noticing a cabinet with double locks. "What's this?" I ask, pointing to it.

"In case you need to lock up your vitamins or something. It's locked for security.

"We'll have to move it out of this room, but I love the idea." I look around in astonishment, not believing my eyes.

"You like it?" Dante asks.

"I love it. Thank you so much for making this happen." I walk up and give him a hug.

He chuckles before placing a soft kiss on the top of my head. There's a knock on the door and I do a little skip towards it. Dante, like the over-protective man he is, strolls ahead of me to answer the door, until I call his name. "Dante."

His one eyebrow lifts in questioning. "What are you doing? You scare the shit out of these women. Go hide in the bathroom for a second." I shoo him away, as he gives me a *you got to be kidding* look, but does as I ask.

One of the ladies I've been treating walks in, folding in half. "Has your water broken yet?" I ask, immediately getting into midwife mode.

"Yes," she half yells, half moans in pain.

"How far apart are your contractions?" I grab a big workout ball she can use to sit on to help her labor. Her hand goes to her stomach as I help her onto the ball. Her body knows what to do as soon as she sits down and her legs naturally bounce.

"Three to four minutes apart."

I look around the space and in a few cabinets, before running to the bathroom. "Dante, I need a slow cooker to keep water warm, and face cloth," I whisper.

"I'll text my guy, unless I can come out now?" I shake my head, mentally starting to make a list of what I'll need.

"You taking charge right now is sexy as Hell," Dante whispers into my ear.

Trying to stay professional, I ignore his flirting, and return back to the task at hand. "Lorna, you're doing great." I rub her back trying to soothe her pain. "Remember, each contraction is one step closer to meeting that precious baby of yours. Let the contractions do the work."

She breathes deeply through another set of contractions. "I've been visualizing this moment, just like you told me to," she says, strained, but overall, much calmer than she was when she walked in. "I was so scared you wouldn't be here. I came earlier but you weren't open yet."

Over the next few hours, Dante's men bring me a few items I need to help with a home-like birth, but never try to walk in. I'm running on adrenaline and the high I get from helping others.

Once I have Lorna moved into the room, I allow Dante out of the bathroom. He has rolled up his sleeves and helped with every request I've given him. He even looks like he's enjoying himself.

I bring a healthy baby girl into the world and it serves as another reminder of how much I miss my daughter. I glance over at Dante, who peeks through the small space between the door and the wall, and he gives me a wink, before stepping back.

My smile spreads across my face and I'm once again consumed with how Dante makes me feel.

I hand the newborn to Lorna. I step out of the room to see Dante, giving the mother privacy as she bonds with her daughter.

I pull my gloves off and dump them in the trash. "She shouldn't leave here for at least twelve hours." I look in the direction of the room before wiping some stray hairs away from my face with the back of my hand. "But I would have to stay with her..." My words linger as I ask for permission without asking.

"What are you asking me for, Demi?" he asks softly.

I walk to the sink and wash my hands. "Do you mind if I stay with her and miss my shift?" I finish rinsing my hands before I look back at Dante. My heart is in my throat as I wait for his answer.

His lips purse and I can't tell what he's thinking. "I have a meeting. I can't stay."

I nod, refusing to feel disappointed. I already knew the answer before I asked it. I plaster a fake smile on and go to stand by him.

"But I'll leave you with my phone and a guard to keep an eye on things outside until I can come back," he says before pulling me in for a kiss.

"Really?" My eyes widen with surprise.

"You did a great thing tonight and you need to see it through."

Dante tenderly cups my jaw with his hand. It's sweet and caring, the complete opposite of the man he is in public. "Thank you."

I lean in and press my lips to his. Our kiss is everything we aren't and our world can never be: soft, sweet, kind.

He pulls away and I'm still leaning toward him. I'm light headed on endorphins and never want to be away from him.

"Tonight was like nothing I've ever experienced before. Seeing you in your element gives me a whole new appreciation for what you've done in your life. Everyone can see that splash of sparkle you give out to the people you meet. It's magical and everything I knew you could be." He pulls out his phone. "Here's my phone. Call the club if you need anything."

A knock on the door has both our heads turning and it's one of his men. "Boss, have her take mine. Then she can call you directly." One of his men holds up his phone in offering.

"Good idea." Dante takes the phone, placing it in my hands. "Don't hesitate to call me if you need me." He presses a quick peck to my cheek. "I'll be back as soon as I can." He walks out and pauses. "All you have to do is call me or step outside and someone will be here for you."

The phone burns in my hands. All I want to do is call Oakleigh. "Thank you." Dante shuts the door.

I rush to the washroom, locking myself in the small room, and sit on the toilet seat. My hands shake as I call my mother, praying I get to hear my daughter's voice. Even though his man is outside, I'm still scared that if I make this call in the open I'll be found out.

Chapter 24

Demi

"A DRESS ARRIVED FOR you, Demi!" One of the girls calls from near the front door. My hand pauses with my lipstick halfway to my lips as I pull my eyes away from the mirror. A *dress? For what?*

They bring a white box with a purple bow into Tanya's and my room and we both get up at the same time. She plucks the card from the bow, ripping part of the rectangle paper as I take the package. Frustrated with her overstep, I roll my eyes.

She reads the card aloud for everyone. "A dress for the fundraiser. Be ready in one hour."

Her words fall on deaf ears as I open the box and pull out a gorgeous, silky, purple, elegant dress. Its material easily slips from the box and drifts toward the ground as I hold it up with admiration. It has to be from Dante. Then it clicks. He needed a date for a fundraiser. This has to be for that. I'd forgotten all about it since so much time had passed since he talked about it. My stomach flutters with anticipation.

"Good thing we're the same size," Tanya says happily while clapping her hands. "Now your night is free to go to the inner city and help all those women you like."

I stand, stupidly staring at her, not sure what she's talking about. I have never felt anything so soft in my fingers. My eyes drift back to the garment. It's the most beautiful dress I've ever seen. I hug the material closer to my chest.

"It's the event Dante needed a date for, remember? You said I could go in your place." Her brows are raised as she talks to me like I'm stupid.

"That was over a month ago." I'm suddenly excited to go and I want to be the one wearing the dress.

Robin gives me a look but doesn't say anything as she closes the door behind her to allow Tanya and I to fight this out ourselves.

"Of course you would go back on your word," Tanya scoffs. "You sure know how to make friends. Just remember we sleep in the same room, and you're a deep sleeper."

Is that a threat? "Fuck off Tanya. The dress is mine." I pause, before stepping closer to her. My eyes narrow. "Don't threaten me unless you plan to follow through, because I don't make idle threats."

The only time Tanya is kind is when I do something for her. Allowing her to go in my stead would put her in a good mood for two, maybe three days, max. Every time I think I've made progress with starting a friendship, she flips the moment I refuse to do what she wants.

"If Dante sent me the dress, he'll be expecting me to wear it." I hold it flush to my chest.

Tayna steps closer, challenge shining in her eyes. "Oh, please. He doesn't care if it's you or me, honey. All he wants is someone looking nice on his arm."

My molars grind and my lips purse as we glare at each other.

"Now that that's settled..." She grabs my dress and my hands refuse to let go. We both tug on it before I reluctantly release my grip, not wanting to tear the damn thing in half. Stunned by the altercation, I watch as she heads into the bathroom, locking the door behind her.

Oh hell no!

I refuse to allow my eyes to tear. I've never had a brand-new dress before. I tell myself it doesn't matter though; in the end, that dress can't change my life.

Going into my makeup bag, I grab a small brow shaping scissors. The first thing I do is cut a hole in her favorite work outfit before I take my time finishing my makeup. When Dante shows up and I'm not in that dress he's going to be furious. For once, I look forward to seeing this side of him.

Instead of staying hidden in our room, I go into the main living space. All the girls are there, observing how I'm reacting. I go grab a cup of water, down it, before I face them.

"Want company when you go into the city?" Robin asks, and a few others express that they would like to come and help too. None of them are even concerned about the wrath Dante is going to rain down.

"The bus leaves in half an hour, which will allow us to see Tanya off." A forced smile lifts my lips. It hurts and takes more energy than I would like to keep it in place. In the back of my mind there is a small part that questions if Tanya is right and Dante won't care.

Tanya is a ball of energy, gloating through the house once she's finished dressing. Our doorbell rings and all the girls squeal, getting caught up in the moment. I envision cutting her hair while she sleeps. It helps put a real smile on my face.

A sarcastic chuckle leaves me as I realize I've had it way too easy if I'm pouty over something like this.

Dante steps into the room and the air in my lungs vanishes. He's in a tuxedo, his hair is styled, and his scent washes over the entire room. The chatter of the girls dies and the house quickly falls silent. His calloused gaze locks on mine. It's like those dark irises are trying to penetrate my heart to grasp hold of it.

I step back, not liking how his look is heating my skin, or the way my panties dampen.

"Why the fuck are you not in my dress?" he demands, his tone dripping with dominance. His attention is solely on me. I don't even think he's noticed Tanya.

I shiver, never having that tone used toward me before. He steps closer and I step back, bumping into a girl with my back. She quickly gets out of the way, but my feet are now rooted in place.

He leans closer, towering over me as his lips touch my ear lobe. My pulse flickers faster at his closeness.

"Demi?" He curls a small piece of hair around his finger and tugs, drawing me in to have his lips touch my skin. "I've had a shitty day and this is not making it any better." He brings out a gun and traces the cool metal of the barrel over my cheek, slowly dragging it down my skin. I've never seen him hold a weapon before. It's like I've never seen this side of Dante.

I should be scared as fuck, but it does the opposite. I'm beyond turned on.

What is wrong with me?

His back is now to the girls and they have made themselves scarce, disappearing completely from the room. Even Tanya has left, leaving us alone. His gun continues its trail down my body, rubbing over my breast, down my stomach, and stopping between my thighs.

My breathing is the only sound to be heard as the room closes in around us. He slips the pistol under my maxi dress and brushes it back and forth over my panties.

"If I wanted Tanya to come, I would have asked her. I refuse to allow for the girls I own to disrespect me by not doing as I demand. I've been patient with you, understanding even, but now I realize I've shown you too much kindness. You're the only person to ever go against what I have said and it turns out, I'm not fond of the behavior."

The friction between my legs has me wanting to close my eyes. My breathing becomes more like pants and I can't lower their volume.

"Now tell me, will you ever go against my orders again?"

He's watching me with such intent, his expression refusing to soften. My hips move with his rhythm, no matter how much I chastise myself.

"No." I try to shake my head, but he tightens his hold on my hair.

"No, what?" he asks.

Another brush of the gun. Why does this feel so damn fantastic? I should be shitting myself, not about to orgasm.

"No, Sir?"

His lips push against my neck and he nips at my skin. "It's no, Master, to you."

I want to refuse, but his gun stops, and my hips continue trying to work my clit into a frenzy like a junkie needing their next fix. If orgasms are the addiction that kill me, so be it.

"No, Master." I'm hardly able to say it.

His gun moves again and my body explodes in warmth. Light dances behind my eyes. "Don't you dare hold back, or I'll fuck you right here for all of them to hear."

I allow for an unladylike moan to escape my throat and ride the orgasm for all it's worth.

"Good girl."

"Dante," I pant, my legs shaking from the sudden rush.

He pulls the gun from under my dress and I'm suddenly self-conscious of what just happened.

Tanya walks back into the room as if she had her ear on the door waiting for me to finish. She puts on a fake smile for Dante but levels me with an angry glare.

"Your dress, Demi." She hands me the garment as if she hadn't been the one who demanded to wear it.

An Escalade is waiting for us when we step outside. Neither Dante nor I speak as I float between post-orgasm bliss and embarrassment.

After a long, silent drive, we pull up to a dark alleyway.

"This is the place?" I ask, confused. The area is dark and the building nothing like the fancy venue I had envisioned.

"I was going to do this with you, but I changed my mind."

I cock my head, confused about what he's talking about. He opens the door, latching onto my hand, practically dragging me out of the car.

"I'm not the pushover boy I was back then. *This* is who I am now."

He opens the door to the run down building and it makes a piercing noise before slamming shut with an echoing *thud* behind us. I jump closer to Dante and he links our fingers together, leading me deeper into the darkness.

"This is where I do bad things," he whispers into my ear. "I'm nothing like the boy you once knew."

I swallow down my nerves, my fingers tightening around his.

"If you're doing bad things, it's for a reason. You're the most level-headed person I know." I know what he's trying to do. He can't scare me away.

"You need to meet more people," he teases, before growing more serious. "I've never been a good person."

"People may perceive you as a monster but you've always been a good man to me."

He scoffs. "Don't be making excuses for me. Have you paid attention to anything since you've come into my life? My brother is the Don of the Mancini family, I buy women from auctions, and I'll never hesitate to hurt anyone who threatens my way of life. I've worked too hard to get where I am today."

"The club girls look at you like you're their savior. They would die for you," I argue back, not understanding how he can't see himself like I do.

"You don't see the irony in the fact that *owning* those girls is the only good thing I've ever done?"

Dante lets go of my hand and turns on a light. A large board covered with pictures greets me. My eyes immediately narrow in on Jameson's picture, among the many others.

"What's this?"

"This is the trafficking ring I'm deeply involved with."

I look back at the board, recognizing Tex's picture, the man who sold me to Dante, and a few others I have seen around Jameson. My stomach dips and rolls, and I wish I had a candy to pop into my mouth.

I walk toward Dante, wrapping my arms around his neck. "My outcome would have been vastly different if you weren't involved with that. I'm grateful for you." I glance back at the board and my heart refuses to allow me to imagine Dante's picture beside the others. He's not like them.

"You're the exception, Demi." He untangles my arms and scratches his head. "I've watched innocent lives be ruined."

"No, you're the exception. You have morals and a kind heart."

"You don't know the things I've done and how good I sleep after."

"I don't need to know what you've done. How many other women have you helped?"

His eyes drift from the board to a chair in the middle of the room. "I killed a man here not long ago. I enjoyed every second. To have that much power in your hands is a slippery slope. It's not long before I will crave it. I see how my brothers are and I know this is only the beginning."

I use my fingers on his jaw to turn his head until he's looking at me and place my hand over his chest. "It's what's in here that matters. Your heart is made of gold. I've never cared about anything else. People like us don't have the luxury of thinking further than what's right, and the way we get there is often a little gray."

Dante is devastatingly hot and intimidating. His expression fluctuates between crazed killer and church boy while he evaluates my reaction. I lick my lips and his eyes track the movement with a predatory focus, flashing with darkness. It's a darkness I recognize, as I also have it within myself, and it reminds me that we can never escape our past and the way it shaped us.

"The ugliness of our world has never scared me and I refuse to let it start doing so now," I assure him.

He looks like he wants to believe me but uncertainty waivers in his eyes. "Our past has only made you more beautiful, Demi. It's refreshing for someone to understand me and know where I'm coming from." His hands link through mine and, with unapologetic conviction, he adds, "I'll never hesitate to protect what's mine, no matter the cost."

He's searching deep within my morally gray soul for something, and he must see it. The one side of his lips lift into a smirk and he squeezes my hand. "Let's get this stuffy party over and done with so we can go home."

Chapter 25

Dante

WE WALK INTO THE fundraiser fashionably late. My family; Romeo, his wife Gia, Savio, his wife Charlotte, Max, and some random woman I've never met before, all sit at a round table with two empty seats.

"Dante!" Romeo stands to greet us, shaking my hand.

"Romeo, this is Demi. Demi, my brother Romeo." I make quick introductions around the table while my brother's eyes stay on Demi. It's never a good thing to be on Romeo's radar for long.

I don't get nervous often, but right now the tension has my molars grinding.

"Demi, you and my wife have a few things in common. I think you girls will get along well," Romeo offers and the tension leaves my bones.

We take a seat, the table growing awkwardly silent. I watch Demi take a drink of her water before clearing her throat. "What type of fundraiser is this?"

"It's supporting a nonprofit organization that fights against human trafficking," I reply, watching for her reaction. She chokes on her water and I rub at her back. After our conversation at the warehouse, I've decided that tonight will be the night that I trust her with my biggest secret. She has no idea how deeply involved I really am with trafficking. "It's great networking," I add with a smirk.

"I hear you and Dante knew each other in high school," Charlotte says, trying to gain Demi's attention. I'm grateful for her trying to include her.

Once the women are in conversation, Romeo nods his head and the men at the table stand. We follow him like good little soldiers and the thought has me chuckling to myself. Savio narrows his eyes at me, already knowing what I'm thinking, while Max keeps his eyes on the room. He has this creepy fucking grin on his face. He's the one guy in this world I would be scared of if I got on his bad side. From the stories I've heard, he's fucking crazy, but who am I to judge?

We head to the bar to gather drinks for ourselves. "What's up?" I ask.

Instead of Romeo speaking, Savio answers. "Tomorrow, Charlotte is announcing that the Bratva are not the only ones with the one-of-a-kind diamonds." His voice is hushed as he makes sure no one is listening to us. I watch as his whole body vibrates with energy and excitement.

Charlotte's father is the head of the Bratva, the Russian mafia, and specializes in selling diamonds. Charlotte left her family for my brother, Savio, and took part of the empire with her. We're already at war with them, and this news will only serve to elevate things to a whole new level of hostility.

I can feel eyes on my back and glance behind me, half expecting Demi to be coming my way, but she's still at the table, her attention fully on the conversation. She looks beautiful and seems to be getting along with the other women. It's important that the others like her.

As if sensing my eyes on her, she turns around and catches me staring at her. Her face lights up and my heart does a double thud.

"I didn't want to mention this with the girls around, but mother showed up at my gate this morning," Romeo adds.

My muscles tense at the mention of our mother. The scarred cross over my pec stings like it was burned into me only yesterday. "What the hell did she want?"

"She looked like she was high off something and kept repeating herself."

"What did she say?" I ask again, annoyed he ignored the question.

"She was spewing some shit about Demi and kept saying she had photos to prove it."

That woman is never happy unless the whole world is burning.

"What was she saying about Demi?" I try to control the rage burning in me. The only way she would know that Demi is back in my life is if she's keeping tabs on us.

"Honestly, I don't know. I couldn't follow along, didn't want to. I sent her away with a few hundred bucks to give us time to do something about her."

"She needs to greet our father in Hell," Savio responds, looking just as angry as I am.

"If you're not ordering a drink, move so that others can." The annoyed female voice comes from behind us and we all turn, unimpressed, to find Sienna standing there with a big ass grin on her face. I watch as Max takes his time looking her up and down before he switches his smile into the less crazy, more charming one.

She steps in, giving me a hug. I freeze and shoulder her arms off me. She mouths *sorry* and turns her attention to my brothers. It's not uncommon for her to join me for functions like these, and they all know her.

"Babe, when you said you couldn't come with me tonight, I asked someone else," Maximus cockily responds.

"Yes, I met her earlier. Lovely girl." She turns her body to dismiss my brother. "Dante, I want you to meet my date."

I suck in my lips, trying not to laugh in my brother's face. I extend my hand to the silent tall guy behind her.

"Not him." She rolls her eyes and this time, Max is the one laughing. "He's over there." She points.

I glance over and what I see has my knuckles turning white as my fingers try to crush the glass in my hands. Jameson. The one guy I should have crushed when I had the opportunity. I haven't seen him in the flesh for a decade and most traces of the young man in the photo on my board have vanished.

Everyone is looking at me oddly and I realize my face has just revealed a side of me I try to keep hidden. My lips lift into a gentle smile, the muscles fighting against the action. My brothers relax, except Savio, but I appreciate the mask of indifference he wears. I'm going to hear about it from him once we're away from prying eyes and ears.

"I'm going to go do my big brother thing for Sienna. I'll be back," I tell the guys before I stroll over to Jameson.

"I'll keep her in good company until you return," Max offers, taking Sienna's arm to lead her away.

"I'll distract Demi for you," Savio replies, having my back like the good brother he is.

My walk is stiff and Jameson looks all too pleased with himself when he sees I'm coming to him.

"I didn't realize they allowed riff raff in here," I say, my polite tone a stark contrast to the words.

He extends his hand and my eyes glance down before they flick back to hold his gaze. I refuse to mirror his motion, unwilling to shake his hand. He looks like a snake waiting for an opportunity to strike.

"You need to fucking leave." My lips pinch together.

He makes a show of leaning past me, looking at Demi, then fixes his eyes back on me. "I think I'll stay." He flashes me a cheeky grin that I want to punch off his face.

My hand dips into my suit jacket and I show him my gun, hoping to scare him off.

"I can play at this game too." He does the same thing with his suit and gun.

My fingers interconnect, and I crack a few of my knuckles.

"You have no fucking clue, do you?" His tone is taunting. The urge to shoot him dead in the middle of this room is digging deeper into my skin.

"I can kill you, with a hundred people around, and no one will remember seeing anything that happened. They won't even recall me being here."

"I can't leave my date, that would be rude of me." He shows me his perfectly white teeth, but they're crooked as hell.

I glance over my shoulder and Max has Sienna up against a wall with his hands caging her in.

"I'd say, your date has forgotten about you already." I step up and remove my gun, resting it above his heart. "You need to forget you ever saw Demi, and never contact Sienna again. Otherwise, I'll bury you."

I nudge my gun against him and nod toward the exit. "I'm not your enemy here, Dante. Demi doesn't deserve the pedestal you have always placed her on. You'll see what I'm talking about soon enough." He turns and heads toward the exit by our table.

"You're going out the back door." I place my hand on his shoulder and move him where I want. He doesn't argue or fight.

"We'll see each other soon, Dante." He takes a step before he pauses and turns back around. "Here's where I'm staying, just in case you want to chat more." I accept a card from some shitty motel close to the neighborhood I grew up in.

My fingers itch to blow his head off, even though I'm not the violent one in our family. I wait until his back disappears into the night's darkness before I alert our security so that Jameson doesn't return.

I walk back to the table after the speeches have already started. "Where's Max?" He and his date are not at the table.

Savio shrugs. I look around the room and notice Sienna is also nowhere to be seen.

"You, okay?" Demi asks, placing her hand on my thigh to give me a small squeeze.

My hand covers hers. "I just had to deal with business."

She tries to move her hand from under mine, but I keep it in place. We stare into each other's eyes and I have no idea what she's searching for in mine. I can't help but wonder if she knew Jameson would be here tonight.

"Did your business matter include another woman?" she asks, taking a sniff of my jacket. I smell the same spot and realize Sienna's perfume lingers. Jealousy sparks in her irises. It looks good on her, and because I'm a bastard I refuse to answer. I want to wrap her in this state forever.

A small grin graces her perfect lips as she tries to hide the jealousy.

"The only woman I want to enjoy tonight is you," I whisper in her ear, putting her out of her misery. Again, she tries to remove her hand and again, I refuse to allow it.

She turns her head and shifts her body to ignore me and listen to the speakers. Her free hand plays with her hair, moving it from one side and exposing her delicate skin that I would love to nip.

"You mad at me, Demi?" My hand trickles down her arm and goosebumps scatter across her skin. Leaning into her, my lips pull at her earlobe. "We both know you can never stay angry at me long."

She smells delicious, a soft vanilla scent envelopes me.

"I have no reason to be upset. It's your active imagination playing tricks on you. Did you *want* me to be mad at you?" The sass spewing from her fuckable lips has my cock hardening.

I wrap my arm around her, pulling her chair closer to me. "I'm just trying to be a gentleman, and put your feelings first. That's all."

She scoffs with a roll of her eyes.

"You looking for a spanking? Because that eye roll has my hands twitching."

"That sounds ungentlemanly." Her tone is unimpressed but her eyes sparkle with the idea.

"It's not. You'll enjoy it and come so hard you'll make my leg wet."

"You're disgusting."

"We both know that if I slipped my hand up your dress right now, I'd find you wet. It's a lot easier to embrace your desires than fight them."

She squirms under my arm, pleasing me.

"I'm going to fuck you tonight." This girl has me breaking all of my rules. I've never fucked any of my club girls until her. My dick is refusing to think of her as one of them. Since she's walked back into my life, my cock refuses to work unless it's for her. No other woman even makes it twitch anymore. It refuses to come to life unless I imagine her, which I spend an awful lot of my alone time doing.

She rests her shoulder into my side. "Not happening."

I can't see her face anymore, but I bet she's wearing a smug grin.

"It *will* be happening, and you're going to beg for my cock before I give it to you. The more you sass back, the more you'll have to beg."

"You're delusional." Her comeback is weak and she knows it.

I can play this game. I'm the one who wrote the rules.

Chapter 26

Demi

Over a hundred thousand dollars were donated tonight at the fundraiser. It's hard not to feel a tinge of jealousy. My mind keeps dreaming up ways I could use just a few thousand. I could afford to get Oakleigh into that new experimental group that shows promise. I would never have to ration medication that was never meant to be rationed.

I could desperately use a fraction of that money.

But then I feel bad for even thinking about it. The money is going to help women survive and beat the odds when everything else feels lost.

"Don't say a word and keep your eyes down at all times," Dante's rough voice brings me back to the present.

"Dante, my boy!" I instantly recognize the man from the front row of my auction. My stomach crawls with the way he's looking at me. Quickly, I cast my eyes down. "I'd say good to see you, but every time we meet up, you take what I want. If I were a self-conscious man, I'd say you do it on purpose."

Dante laughs, shaking his hand. "It's your competitive nature. If this one is still in good shape when I'm done, you can have her, Capella."

"Now you're just teasing me. Everyone knows once they hit your hands, no one will ever see them again."

"I like to get my money's worth," Dante responds. I can't believe they're openly talking about trafficking girls at a place like this. Everyone in the room has donated and vowed to help.

The man walks away and two of Dante's fingers lift my chin.

"I just don't understand," I say.

He interconnects our fingers and leads us away from the table, past the bar, toward the elevators. We stay silent. The doors ding open, we step in.

I wait for him to push me against the wall and kiss me, making good on his promise, but he doesn't.

The doors ding again and he leads me to a hotel room.

"Can I trust you?" he asks.

I nod, my hands grow clammy at the unknown.

He swipes a plastic key over the lock and it lights green before he ushers me in and closes it behind us.

"What have you brought us tonight?" Two men in cheap-looking suits stand looking at me.

My fight-or-flight response kicks in and I try to turn back around, but Dante keeps me in his strong hands. "Gentlemen, this is Demi Gallo."

My heart races. These guys' hair is styled back with too much gel, they have creepy mustaches, and look like the type that might offer candy to children.

"She's not our usual type. They're typically younger." They sound disappointed.

"Do you want me to stay?" Dante asks. My mouth drops, not believing he would leave me alone in here.

"Yeah, stay and observe, maybe you can help a little."

I try to swallow the saliva building in my mouth. It takes a second time to shove it all the way down my throat. Dante pushes me deeper into the room.

"She's in good condition. She must have cost a penny."

It takes a second for me to find my backbone. "She has a name. It's rude not to use it."

They look shocked at my outburst. The men's eyes fly to Dante.

"She willingly entered the auction," Dante sighs, gesturing toward me with his hand.

Now they look impressed.

"What the hell is this?" I ask, placing a hand on my hip.

"Demi, this is special agent Barnes and special agent Horne. They're undercover, trying to bring down one of the largest trafficking rings in the world."

I look back at Dante. "I'm so confused."

He wraps his arm around my shoulder, his warmth radiating through my body, sinking deep into my bones. When he does this, no matter the situation, I feel safe. False security, I'm sure of it, but my body refuses to see reason.

My heart is still racing as I try to relax.

"Demi, can you tell us who your contact was to get into the auction?" Special agent Horne asks.

I look up at Dante, who nods his head. "We can trust these guys. I've been working with them for the last six years. Together, we have saved about a thousand women as I enter deeper into the trafficking world. I'm their inside guy."

I should have expected this, but I never saw it coming. "If you save women, why am I working for you?"

The men glance at Dante, then at me. Dante stiffens beside me.

"Stop asking questions, and answer theirs, Demi." His tone is full of authority, ignoring what I asked.

"A guy named Tex. I begged him to let me enter," I answer.

"How do you know Tex?"

I glance up at Dante once again. I hate how it looks like I need his approval before I answer anything. I'm just worried about saying Jameson's name out loud. Dante's mood always changes whenever I do.

"No one will know you said anything." They think I'm worried about giving up my source. I'm not. I'm worried about how it will affect Dante and I.

"Jameson."

"Does Jameson have a last name?"

"Jameson Kelly."

"How do you know him?" Agent Horne asks.

How do I tell them the truth? At this point, where do I even start?

"He grew up in the same small town as us," Dante answers for me.

"Do you have a picture of him?"

I shake my head.

"I can get you one," Dante adds.

They question me for an hour before Dante and I leave the room. My mind is spinning, and I feel exhausted.

"I still don't know, are you helping or not?" I ask.

He wraps his body around me, pulling me into a hug. "I'm trying to take down the largest human trafficking ring in the world. I regularly buy women and set them up with new identities and a new life. Each woman has helped to fill in the blanks for us, giving us a clearer picture of our target. The longer I'm in that circle, the more help I can give. Only those two men know my real purpose. Everyone else thinks I'm vicious. It *has* to stay that way or I lose all my power."

"I don't deserve you." I shake my head. "You are a better person than me."

"Not true. I love everything about you."

He leads me back to the main room and takes me out onto the terrace. As soon as the few people out here see Dante, they quickly leave, allowing us some privacy.

I keep my voice low. "I thought the mafia doesn't work with the cops?"

"This isn't me working with them. We help each other, that's all. You will never find me on a stand in court. They respect that I deliver justice in a different method than they can. If they could, they would use me and toss me in jail."

I shiver from the cooler night air and he wraps his arm around me.

"I want to help too," I say leaning back into him.

"And you have. You already gave us more information than we had before." Dante's voice is soft, his thumb circling on top of my hand.

I turn into his embrace. "I want to do what you do and go undercover to help."

He's staring down at me softly. It's like we've been transported ten years into the past. He's looking at me like I mean everything to him. It lights my skin on fire and warms my heart. Dante has been the only person to ever look at me like I am worth more than anything else in the world.

I rise on my tiptoes, wanting to kiss him. One hand gently cups the side of my jaw as the other threads through my hair. Taking his time, he dips his head to close the distance between us. I shut my eyes, anticipation strumming through me. His touch, his kisses, are the most intoxicating thing I have ever had. My lips are warmed by his breath fanning across them, energy radiates off them as he takes his time teasing me. I'm about to open my eyes to see if he plans on kissing me sometime this century, when he finally lowers his lips to mine.

They are more delicious than I remember. I lose myself in his touches as he kisses me like he's a starved man and I'm the cure to his hunger. My heart wants to burst, with its newfound warmth of love.

I have loved this man since I was seventeen years old. The thought slams into me like a sledgehammer and I pull away, catching my breath. I want to cry for how I've treated him our entire lives. I always pushed him away when I should have been holding onto him tighter. The fact he's still here, holding me, is a miracle.

"Why are you so kind to me?" I ask, my guilt beginning to consume me like it does every time before I force myself to place distance between us.

"Your heart is bigger than everyone's in there. It's something to be cherished."

It's things like this that amplify the guilt I harbor. "You can't say things like that to me."

"Why?"

"I've always thought I never deserved you. When you say nice things, it sends me into a spiral where I think you're better off without me in your life." There, I said part of the truth that has plagued me for years. My chest hurts from the radical pounding of my heart.

"So, you would rather I be an ass?"

He's staring at me with sadness in his eyes. This is why I've never said anything before.

"Forget I said anything." I try to push away from him—to hide my heart—and I wish I could disappear into the shadows.

"Don't do that." His fingers circle my wrist and he pulls me snug to him. "I know you can't control how you feel, but I wish you could see yourself through my eyes. You are perfect. I tell you nice things like this because I hope that, if you hear them enough, one day you might believe in them. Even if it's only for thirty seconds, it's a start."

Tears pepper my eyes. I was taught to be stronger than this. Dante kisses my forehead, then my closed eyes, before placing a kiss to my lips. It's soft and quick, the barest of whispers, before he's back staring into my soul through my eyes.

"I know about all the dark things we had to survive growing up," he whispers.

I shake my head because he doesn't know what happened after he left. It gets stuck in my throat and my body shakes, trying to push it out. He wraps his arms around me tighter, holding me, not saying a word.

"I need you to punish me." My words are hardly audible and I disappoint myself when they cover up the truth.

"No, Baby Girl. I'm going to worship you." His tone is strong and lethal and I refuse to argue. "Now ask me nicely."

"What?" He gives me enough room to look up at his face.

"Ask me nicely to worship your body." That cocky smirk of his is back in place.

"Will you please worship my body?"

He shakes his head. "You don't sound desperate enough to have me feast on your pussy and definitely not enough to have my cock in that sweet cunt of yours."

His dirty words have my self-pity floating away and a new heat crawling into my muscles.

He takes my hand and leads us out of the night and back into the fundraiser room. "Where are we going?"

"You sound disappointed that I'm not bending you over outside."

A shiver rolls through me with anticipation.

"I can't guarantee no one will see you out there and I never share what's mine."

Chapter 27

Demi

He drags me toward the elevators, the door already sitting open. Dante pushes a button before caging me in the moment they close. His hands slide down the length of my body.

"You're going to look so gorgeous on your knees begging for my cock." He places kisses along my neck, capturing me, holding me at his mercy. I elongate my neck, silently begging for more.

The door dings open and I watch as Dante adjusts his large erection through his pants. There's no hiding it as he leads me down a hallway to yet another hotel room door. He slides a plastic key over the lock and opens the room for us.

We enter and the first thing I notice is that one wall is comprised of a window that looks into the room beside it.

"Before you entered my life, I would rather watch than partake in the fun." His voice is low and rumbly, coming from behind me. His fingers feather over my shoulder and down my arm.

"Can they see us?" I turn my neck to see his gorgeous face.

"No, it's a two-way mirror. They see themselves, that's it."

I look back at the window, intrigued, but not liking the idea that anyone could be watched and not know about it.

"You don't have to worry. The people who get that room pay extra for just the chance of someone watching them," Dante answers huskily.

"What about this room?"

"I own this hotel. This room is mine and no one ever stays in it but me."

I walk to the glass and place my hand on it. "Do you want me to go into that room?" I ask, unzipping the back of my dress as I allow the material to pool at my feet.

"No. I like touching you." He hooks his finger into his tie and loosens it before tossing it to the ground.

I watch, memorized, as he leisurely undoes each button as he watches me. The shirt opens with ease and his chiseled stomach sits underneath, begging for my fingers to touch him.

I step out from the material on the ground and close the gap between us. I try to assume the position of a confident woman, but my one hand rests over my stomach. The last time Dante saw me naked, I was a decade younger, I hadn't had a child, and my skin was flawless. Now, I'm marked, and my ass is definitely not in the same position it used to be.

His eyes skim over me and light with delight. It's like he can't see the extra skin, or the zebra-striped pattern on my stomach. He lifts my hand, exposing more skin to him.

"I want you to repeat after me," Dante says before he pulls me in and presses kisses along my neck. I close my eyes, loving the action. No one but him has ever kissed my neck before. The act is intimate and kind, it makes it easy for me to fall down the rabbit hole of wanting what I can't have.

"I am beautiful."

When I don't repeat immediately, he stops, and it has me realizing I need to repeat after him. "I am beautiful." That isn't too hard. I can recognize that I'm not ugly on the outside. My face is pretty enough.

"On the inside."

I wish I was a person who could easily lie, but continuing his sentence is harder than it should be.

"On the inside." My hand rubs above my heart, hating the way it squeezes. Dante has always been one of the good ones in our dark world.

He twirls his finger around in the air to direct my movement as I do a slow turn. A low growl erupts from his throat as he watches me.

Movement across the room catches my attention. Another couple has entered the mirrored room. The man rips her dress in two pieces before picking her up and they both slam into the mirror while they passionately kiss each other.

I jump when I feel Dante come up from behind, his hands wrapping around me. "I can close the curtain."

I shake my head. "No, I want to watch." I've never watched anyone before, not even in porn. My nipples pucker against my strapless bra, the material scratching against their sensitivity. Dante's knuckles move back and forth across the smooth fabric, teasing me.

The other couple is mesmerizing in the way they can't stop touching each other.

A cool breeze brushes against my breast as my bra cup is folded down and Dante's fingers circle my nipple.

His other hand slips down and brushes against my panty covered pussy, while his large erection is pushed against my ass cheeks through his pants. "You like watching as much as I do." His breath is warm against my neck.

I must admit, watching another couple have sex is the most erotic thing I've ever done, but I think my scale is a little skewed compared to his. He rubs at the wet spot on my panties, another reminder that I'm enjoying the show.

"They get off on the idea that someone is watching them. They're putting on a show for us."

He unclips my bra and it falls to the ground. "I thought you planned on me begging tonight."

"Oh, you most definitely will be." His fingers rip my panties away at the same moment the girl in the other room is tossed onto the bed. I suck in a breath, my heart pounding. With no warning, Dante tosses me over his shoulder and drops me onto the bed. He pulls my ankles off the mattress, so his head is between my thighs. I'm in the same position as the other girl.

His hand kneads my thigh before he places a kiss on my labia. My legs are spread wide, and I gasp when his tongue licks my clit.

"I want you to watch him as I eat your pussy."

I rise on my elbows to view the other room, but my attention is continually being drawn back to Dante.

"If I'm going to finish eating, you need to relax," Dante growls, before latching back on to my clit. He sucks on it, hard, and my eyes almost roll backwards. I force them back to the room next to us, watching the other man. He's eating her pussy like he's starving. I glance down at Dante and his actions are similar.

The draw to Dante has been something I could never say no to. When he's near, all I feel is complete. I don't think there's a thing in this world this man could not convince me of. It's scary how much control he has over me. Even when I know it, I can't stop it.

His mouth is magic. It's unrelenting and consuming, filling me with emotions I had forgotten about.

"Dante," I groan. "I need you inside of me."

He cockily looks up, his mouth shining with evidence of me. Never once have I regretted Dante. The only regret is we could never stay on the same path, but I'm the one to blame for that.

He curves two fingers in me and his other hand twists at my nipple before his merciless tongue is back at my clit. Lights burst behind my eyes and I hadn't even realized I closed them. I cry out his name again, my hands threading through his hair.

My hips buck, taking all the pleasure he's willing to give. I want to feel him deep inside me. He kisses the sides of my thighs as he stands between my legs. I watch him push down his pants, boxers and all. His cock springs out, pointing straight up. I swear he's gotten larger than he used to be. His dick is thick and veiny, looking smooth with no hair.

The heat from our little escapade drifts away and the cooler air rushes down over my naked body. When it hits my stomach, I already know I plan to tell him the first part of my secret. It's not like I could ever keep anything from him, anyway. He has a way of making me confess to all my sins, even when I don't want to.

A small bundle of nerves sticks to my throat and I'm left staring at Dante's dick because if I catch his eye, he'll know I'm keeping a secret.

"I thought you tasted like candy back then, Demi. I forgot you are the most delicious thing in this world."

My heart is beating out of control. I move to my knees on the bed and grasp his cock. "Only this cock knows how to make me come." It's the painful truth. "Fuck me with it. Remind me what I've been missing."

My eyes prickle with unshed tears that I try to blink away as I look down, watching myself stroke him hard, twice, before his hand covers mine. His other hand tilts my face up. Thank goodness, I've blinked away my emotions.

"I told you, I'd have you begging tonight." His cocky, happy-go-lucky smile cuts through the tension in my body.

Diving forward, he presses his lips against mine. His legs sprawl over my lower half, with the head of his cock at my entrance, causing all my thoughts to evade me. I squirm, wanting him, and lift my hips. He pushes into me in one smooth motion. I gasp, not used to his size. He rocks his hips hard and fast, just how I like it. My hands cling to his shoulders as I hold on for the ride.

"Demi," he whispers between kisses, while my whole body gives itself over to him.

I link my ankles around his back, his balls slap against my ass while his six-pack rubs at my clit each time he thrusts down into me.

Dante's tongue strokes and prods, devouring my mouth. This is far more intimate than any other time we've ever had sex. My mind, soul, and body have given themselves over to him. He groans animalistically. "This pussy has always been mine. I'm never giving it up now."

We stare into each other's eyes, our connection unwavering. To be connected to Dante Mancini like this gives me a sense of levitating.

He thrusts harder, his hand stroking my neck before he wraps his fingers around it. The pressure is just enough to show me he's in charge. I moan, raking my fingers down his back, remembering how much he used to like it. His eyes close and he groans, his back arching into me. My core tightens, and I'm on the brink of another orgasm. He thrusts again, circling his hips, and I'm a goner. My nails rake harder against his back as I scream out his name.

He quickly pulls out, his cum coating my stomach as he orgasms. I fall back, exhausted, and fully content.

"You take my breath away," Dante compliments, but I'm too tired to disagree with him. His cum is sticky on my skin and I don't want it to dry on me. I lean over to grab my torn panties to clean it off when Dante moves my hand away and cleans it with his shirt.

He doesn't pause at my scars, and I wish he would, and push the subject.

He lays down on the bed with me and I snuggle into his side. "When you asked me to run away with you, I was pregnant." He stills under me, but it feels so good to tell the truth.

I take a deep breath, my chest heaving. It's still hard to talk about. "The plan was to tell you when I came back, but we both know how that went."

He's frozen, but I can hear him breathing deeply beside me. My hand instinctively touches my stomach. "I couldn't keep them safe and ended up losing the baby." It's so hard not to slip back into that dark part of my life. I was so depressed after losing the only thing that could give me a reminder of Dante.

Chapter 28

Dante

My hand slides on top of Demi's stomach. I never noticed her blemished skin, until just now. A baby caused these marks. The thought never slipped into my mind. Fuck, a baby never crossed my mind. It should have. We rarely used a condom, because I never wanted anything between us. Our skin-to-skin contact always brought us closer, and I would have hated losing that part of us.

"Move back in with me." I've been in agony since the day she left. I only have my pigheaded self to blame for that.

She blows a breath out. "I don't think that's a good idea." Her voice is uncertain and shaky.

"Why?" *There's no downside.*

"The girls already have a hard time seeing me as an equal. I can't be working at the club *and* living with you."

"Fine, then stop working at the club." *Problem solved.*

She turns to me. "How do I pay off my debt to you?" She sounds pissed.

"I've never cared about that. I don't own you, and you don't owe me money." My chest feels lighter than it ever has. Demi can finally be mine without any unwanted strings attached.

"Why would you do that for me?"

Her beautiful eyes are studying me with skepticism and I have no idea how she could not know that I would do anything for her.

"I'm over-staffed?" I joke with a shrug.

Her body gives me a little nudge.

"Seriously, you're free to do what you want." Instead of her body relaxing into me, kissing me back like I'm her God, she tenses. I sigh, not liking her reaction.

Relax, she's still in your arms.

"Dante..."

I look at her and she has tears that prickle her eyes. One lone tear floods over her thick lashes and my finger scoops it up. "My life has been upheaved so many times. I've been taught to believe that if something is too good to be true, it must be. I just need a moment to adjust."

"Will you move in with me? We can figure out the rest after."

"What if I say no?" She's waiting for me to add strings to the stipulations.

"Then you stay with the girls or I'll help find you a place." Her fingers playfully brush over my chest hair as she thinks. "I'm not trying to trick you."

"I need to be on my own."

My heart beats erratically and she glances down at her hand. No doubt she can feel it.

"I also want to pay for my own place." My mouth opens to tell her I can easily cover her costs. "I would love your help in finding a different job and I'm willing to work from the bottom up." Her voice is soft and tender.

Why can't she see I would do anything for her? She is what makes my life better.

Her fingers move from my chest to outlining the wrinkles in my forehead.

I'm a little stunned. No woman has ever said no to me before. Especially if I'm willing to roll out the red carpet for them.

"I'll help you find a safe place and a job. It's going to take a little time for you to get possession of the new home. Until then, you are always welcome to stay at my place," I concede.

"Thank you." She leans down, placing a warm kiss to my lips. "I'll move in tomorrow until we find a suitable home," she says, while looking at me like I'm her knight in shining armor. I thrive on those looks from her, always have.

Her arm wraps around my chest, and her heart thumps as fast as mine against my side.

Demi

I don't remember closing my eyes, but when I wake, my body is refreshed. There's a new found hope stirring deep inside. I can finally get Oakleigh from my mother's place once we find a home suitable for her. I glance at Dante. He resembles his younger relaxed self when he's sleeping. I look forward to Dante meeting my daughter, and I know I'm going to have to tell him soon about the next secret I've been keeping from him.

I stretch my muscles, and Dante stirs beside me. "Good morning, handsome."

"I could get used to this type of wake up. I've never woken up next to a woman before." He pulls me in for a kiss, not caring about morning breath. I try to not breathe as our lips quickly touch. It takes a second for me to comprehend what he's just said.

"You've never had a woman sleepover before?" I can't help the smile that tilts my lips.

"Never saw the point of it."

"What changed your mind?" I'm a glutton for punishment. I want him to say that it was me.

"Fishing for compliments, Demi?" he teases, and I sink into the crevice of his shoulder.

"You always have had a way to make me feel special." I sigh.

"That's because you are."

Chapter 29

Demi

DANTE DROPS ME OFF at the girls' house to change and pack a few things before he returns to pick me up. All the girls are in the main living space when I walk in. It has me pausing, not expecting every eye to be on me.

"Pretty Woman returns to grace us with her presence," Tanya greets, causing the other girls to laugh.

I wish it wasn't a Monday and they were all working.

"Dante couldn't even care to give you fresh clothes to make the walk of shame easier on you." Tanya glares before she studies her long red nails.

My patience with these girls slips, knowing I'm not staying here anymore.

"It's not like any of you would know. After all, his typical rule is no sleepovers," I gloat even though I hoped my voice wouldn't show it.

"We know this look," another girl points out. "This is the look they all have before no one ever sees them again."

"Girl, Dante just wined and dined you and you've just become disposable," Tanya replies, too excited.

"Careful, Demi, you need him, it's not the other way around," Robin says quietly. The look in her eyes shines with worry, unlike all the other girls.

"If she's stupid enough to sign her own death warrant, let her Robin."

I snap and lunge at Tanya. She pulls my hair while I try to punch her anywhere I can. We end up rolling around on the ground. I refuse to listen to them make up rumors about Dante. The other girls divide in numbers, pulling the two of us apart.

I wipe my mouth and a smear of blood is left on my thumb. "I'm leaving this shitty house. I want more for myself than settling for the easy route." I tear myself from the two girls' grip and march into my bedroom, slamming the door shut.

A second later, it opens and I'm about to ask Tanya to leave me alone when Robin walks in.

"I wish I could say they're all jealous, but we've seen stuff like this happen before." She takes a seat on Tanya's bed as I look over the damage Tanya caused to my face through the mirror.

"I've been watching out for myself since I was in elementary school." *Except when Dante used to be my savior.* "I don't need help from anyone."

"Everyone needs someone. Otherwise, it's easy to get lost." Robin grabs a tissue and dabs at a scrape across her cheek.

"Not me."

"Then why the candy wrappers under your pillow?" she quietly asks, her eyes leveling me with a look. It's the candy I binged the last time I felt helpless, unable to control my fate. "We hear you at night, Demi. It's impossible to keep secrets in a house like this."

"It's nothing I can't handle. I do it when I need the feeling of control. Anyway, it has nothing to do with needing anyone."

Robin's lips purse. "You're a smart girl Demi, everyone needs someone. I just worry you might have chosen the wrong someone."

I refuse to listen to anyone talking badly about Dante, and why the hell is she suddenly trying to be supportive and nice. She was the one who gave me the wrong address. I can't trust a thing that comes from her mouth. She's just like the rest of them.

"I need to pack my shit. I'm moving out and I won't be at work on Tuesday," I say, turning my gaze from the mirror.

Robin nods somberly, standing, and gives me a hug. "I hope to see you one day."

I hug her back. "You will, I promise."

Tanya enters, not caring I might want privacy, and lies on her bed, placing her earphones in her ears to drown out our voices. Robin's forehead crinkles before she shakes her head and looks back at me.

My cheek stings from the nail scratch Tanya inflicted. I grab a makeup wipe and clean my face, putting a small amount of face lotion on the cut. I have nothing else to use. Standing in the doorway, Robin watches me through the mirror. I can tell she wants to say more, but knows I'll refuse to listen.

"When you get back on your feet, let me know so I won't have to worry too much," Robin asks, leaving the room. I nod, looking at her reflection.

All my personal belongings fit into one black school backpack. I can't say I've ever owned more than this. Besides, anything more slows me down. I walk out of the room with my bag slung over my one shoulder and try to ignore the questioning eyes on me.

I'm a little sad I could never fit in with these girls. It would've been nice to have that family aspect that Dante had told me about. Not that it matters...I have my daughter; we're each other's family.

I walk out of the house, not saying goodbye to anyone, and no one says a word to me. Dante's not here yet, but I need to get out of this tiny space and away from those snobby bitches. I stand in front of the small single driveway and lift my face to the sun, the warmth feeling good on my skin. This is a new beginning.

Hopefully this one sticks.

I've had so many over the years, but they never helped me get ahead in life.

A sleek black car pulls into the drive and the man of the hour steps out looking handsome as ever in a fresh crisp suit. He graces me with a smile before it disappears, his long powerful strides come toward me with purpose.

"What the fuck happened?" he asks, moving my chin with his fingers for him to get a look at the scratch from all angles. His hold is hard with possessiveness and I wince under the pressure.

"It's nothing, honestly." I don't know why I'm covering for Tanya. I suppose after years of no one giving a damn, I've learned that no one wants the truth. They want to say they did their due diligence and be on their way.

"Don't lie to me, Demi," he seethes, releasing my chin.

"I can handle myself, Dante." I stand taller, not wanting this to turn into something it's not. His jaw works itself over and back, a vein in his neck flickering as he continues to assess me. The intensity of his look has me caving with a reluctant sigh. "Tanya said a few things about you I disagreed with."

His face snaps to look at the large window at the front of the house. The curtain in front moves like someone just dropped it.

"I took care of it." My hand holds his forearm, but he shakes it off.

"Get in the car," he demands. I stay in place, lifting a brow at his tone. His face softens for a second. "Please," he adds politely.

He narrows his eyes and I do as I'm told. Dante leaves no room for argument with the vicious glare he holds.

I reach for the door as he turns toward the house. I watch his back as he enters and I wonder what's going to happen. My leg bounces with nerves. *What if the house lies about what went down and he believes them over me?* My fingers bounce on the handle, unsure if I should go back in there.

I force myself to stop looking out the window and dig into my bag to find a small candy and unwrap it, tossing it into my mouth. I'm unable to wait for it to dissolve on my tongue before I'm crunching down on it. My hand digs into my bag to grab another one.

Five candies later, Dante walks out. He strides smoothly, looking like he's on a red carpet. The only out-of-place thing is the small old home in the background.

I hold my breath, waiting for him to enter the car. He gets into the back with me and the driver rolls down the partition.

"Have a car sent here to escort Tanya." His voice is full of authority.

His hand rests on mine but he doesn't look at me. He stares into the black partition that has rolled back up. Neither one of us breaks the silence in the car. When we finally stop, my head cranes to look at his beautiful house. How life has changed since I was in high school.

Chapter 30

Demi

A DAY LATER, I swipe my clammy hands down my skirt as I swallow a nervous lump of saliva. I feel like I'm lying to Dante by not telling him about Oakleigh.

We're both standing at the base of his driveway while he talks to his driver and I hold a flier about the listing we're going to view. The paper shows a small one-story home that looks way too nice for me to afford. I push down the hope that wants to claw its way into me.

Dante's conversation ends and he opens the door to the back of the car for me.

"Dante, I need to tell you something."

His happy-go-lucky smile diminishes slightly seeing my nervous face. I'm going to tell him about Oakleigh. He's trusted me with his secret, it's the least I can do.

I try to broach the subject. "First off, this place is way too nice." I wiggle the paper in front of him, trying to come up with a way to tell him. He opens his mouth to argue but I place a finger over his lips. "But it would be nice to find a place that's affordable with two bedrooms."

He shrugs and lets a small, manly chuckle out. "Demi, you can have five bedrooms if you want." He's still not believing me I want to afford the house without his help.

Here goes.

"That's not what I mean. I have a—" He places a hand up, stopping my sentence, lifting his phone to his ear.

"This better be important, Max," he greets, mouthing *I'm sorry* as he walks a few feet away to talk in private.

The driver gives me a warm smile.

Disappointment drives its way into me. I finally had the courage to tell him and he walked away before I could. My courage is quickly dwindling. I take a deep breath, my chest expanding then deflating.

"Don't worry. Mr. Mancini is never late." The driver omits the part that people will change their schedule to accommodate him. I force my smile, not wanting the driver to worry about me. I wave him off, tilting my head to the sun and closing my eyes. *I can do this.*

A hand touches my arm and I jump.

"Didn't mean to scare you. I need to do one errand quickly before we go." He pauses, looking sincere. "It's at the club. You can come or I can have one of my men take you to the first showing. Whichever you would prefer."

"If you don't have time to go today, we can find some different places for another day. Ones not in as nice of an area."

He leans in, placing a kiss on my lips and I melt into him, inhaling his calming scent and enjoying the way he makes me feel.

"They will wait for however long I ask them to."

I'd rather not go to the club, but I also don't want to be a burden. "I don't mind waiting," I hear myself saying. "I can stay in the car." No one will say anything nasty if I'm with Dante.

He gestures with his hand for me to slip into the back. When I do, he takes the seat next to me and our legs touch, even though there's enough space to spread out.

"Do you like kids?" The question slips out before I have time to rationalize it.

"I don't mind Romeo's kids. They're a little spoiled, but I plan to use that as leverage for when I need it one day."

"Leverage?" I'm not following what he means and my stomach suddenly knots.

"Romeo likes to give Savio and I a hard time about having it good while growing up. If he ever crosses the line, I plan to remind him how he's raising his own children. I have no doubt he'll stop giving me a hard time the moment the statement leaves my mouth."

"It's strange to think that you have two more brothers. Growing up, you guys never talked about them, and I just assumed there were just you two."

"That's how our mother wanted it." His face masks over as he talks about his mother. "She would have loved to say she buried all of her children if she could."

"That's the saddest thing I've ever heard." I squeeze his hand before he uncurls his fingers from mine.

"Honestly, I stay away from Romeo's kids as much as possible. I had no positive role models growing up. I began stealing petty stuff by the age of eight, and I had graduated to grand theft auto by the time I reached sixteen. I have nothing to offer but bad advice. Hell, my club will probably be the reason his boys lose their virginity. And the girls, they better not ask me for a job."

"Dante, you know the difference between right and wrong." I refuse to let him talk about himself like he's a monster.

"Demi..." He levels me with a look. "The first time I fucked you was on top of your car after beating a John."

I suck in a breath. I tried to forget about that night. Not because of Dante, but because of what I was willing to do.

"It's not like you came from a better home life than me. We should consider ourselves lucky that we don't have kids. We have no right bringing them up in a world like ours."

I feel sucker punched. "I know the difference between right and wrong, and I'm perfectly capable of loving and protecting an innocent child." My brow begins to sweat, my back ram-rod straight, as I grow more passionate about what we're talking about.

He rubs at his forehead. "I'm not trying to fight. The whole world sees me as this horrible monster who sells women. You know that's not the true me, but no one else does. It's the whole reason why you have a cut across half your face. Kids of my own have never crossed my mind. That's my only point." He takes my hand and kisses my knuckles.

"You're a better person than you think," I reply, still reeling at the thought he doesn't want kids brought up in our world. He kisses my hand again. "You and Savio have been the only people to ever believe in me." I move his hand toward me and turn his hand to kiss it like he did mine. We stare into each other's eyes as our connection flows through us.

Maybe I'll wait a little bit to allow him time to digest our conversation before I tell him about Oakleigh.

The partition rolls down. "Change of plans, go to the house and then we'll go to the club."

"Are you sure?" I ask, studying him.

"This is what's important today, not the club."

We stop at a small house among a line of other well-kept houses. I freeze, looking at the beautiful neighborhood. Kids are out on what appear to be new bikes. They don't act scared or worried, which is so unlike how I grew up, but something I have always wanted for my daughter.

"I'm not getting out." I keep my face looking straight and refuse to look any further. Tears threaten to invade, but I keep them at bay with my jaw tight. There's no way I could afford a place like this. I don't even have a job yet, and I can tell you right now, my qualifications can't afford me this.

Dante drags in a long breath like he's frustrated. I refuse to glance over. I can't let my heart even believe in a place like this, because disappointment is heartbreaking. I don't want to want it.

"Demi." He says my name softly, his hand resting on my thigh, and I move my hand away. "Please, look at me." His finger circles over my pants. "I can be just as stubborn as you. I have the time, I could wait all day."

Reluctantly, I turn my head. His eyes hold mine and, for a second, I get lost in them, forgetting why we're together, forgetting that life exists outside our bubble. My stomach flips the way it always does when he gives me his whole attention, as if I'm the only thing that matters. Life can be so cruel, by dangling everything I want in front of me, but never letting me hold onto it.

"My family owns this area. We make sure it stays safe. The lady who is renting her house is going to visit her daughter, who just had her first grandchild. This is a four-month rental, and we would be doing her a favor by taking it. Give it a chance, that's all I ask. If you hate it, I have ten more places to look at."

He looks so sincere; I don't know if I should believe him. "Where is the lady now?"

"Inside waiting for us. Ask her yourself if you don't believe me."

I look past him at the house. The outside looks better than I ever dreamed. This neighborhood is magnificent. Oakleigh could ride a bike and I wouldn't have to worry about her safety. A tingle of excitement wiggles its way into my chest. I try to push it out, but it refuses to move.

"Come on." Dante's lips tilt up and he knows he has me. His eyes already shine with victory at the mere idea of making me happy.

He steps out, reaching his hand in to help me out. There are real flowers under the window. The glass is unbroken and clean. A small *welcome* flower pot sits on the step.

An older lady steps out with a huge smile. She greets Dante by giving him a quick hug that he stiffens under, but she doesn't seem to notice. "I made you your favorite." She gives him a plastic container of homemade cookies. I watch him interact with this lady and can't help but notice when his softer side shines through. You would never guess he's part of the mafia. It's hard not to imagine us living here as a family. No one has ever held a candle to Dante.

Dante, the gentleman he is, brings me into him and introduces me, making me a part of the conversation. It's all so very normal.

"Demi, it is so nice to meet you. There's no way I could go without you being here. My flowers would die, no one would feed my stray cat or the birds." She lowers her voice and leans in towards me. "The crows like a little wine on Fridays, but you have to be careful not to give them too much or they'll get drunk. Just last week they had too much and I had to protect them from the cat."

She leans back up, smiling at the two of us.

"Why don't you give us the tour, Margaret."

The house is perfect. It has two rooms, a modest kitchen that connects with a living room, and it's all on one floor. Large sliding doors welcome us to the backyard. It's small, but maintained. Everything about this place is perfect.

"What is the rent again? It slipped my mind," I ask Margaret. She glances toward Dante, looking unsure.

"It's just the regular monthly bills like electricity and water that needs to be covered. I would need you to continue with the house upkeep, with watering flowers, cutting the lawn."

This place is too good to be true. I should be saying no, but instead I say, "I'll take it." This gives me four months to save to find another place that would be acceptable.

Dante claps his hands together. "Well, that was easy," he says with a wide grin. We shake hands with the homeowner, saying our goodbyes. My stomach flutters with Dante's hand on my lower back as we walk back to the car.

"You should let me take you shopping to fill up that extra room."

"Dante, stop." I turn and hold my hand up to his chest.

"Fine, one new outfit."

Why does he have to be so nice all the time?

"It's not that." I swipe my hand across my nose and mouth. "The stretch marks on my stomach are from me having a baby nine years ago."

"The miscarriage?" Dante's phone rings and he silences it before placing it back in his pocket.

I shake my head, sucking in my lips as I study his reaction.

"You didn't have a miscarriage?" He scratches at his head. Why is this so hard for me to say? His phone rings once again, its tone loud and grating on my ears.

"After the miscarriage, you were gone. My mother was sleeping twenty-four-seven, I had no one, I was depressed. I was being like her and sleeping all the time. Jameson started to come around and he's the one who convinced me to get out of bed. Shortly after, I found out I was pregnant." I swallow, watching Dante's happiness disappear from his face. "My daughter's name is Oakleigh. She's the whole reason I have to make so much money."

Once again, his phone cuts through the air. "What the fuck do you need, Max?" His eyes stay trained on mine, his facial features hard, sculpting his face like stone. He's silent, listening to his brother. He steps past me, opening the door, and gestures for me to get in.

My fingers pick at the skin around my nail bed as I slide in the back. My heart pounds as I wait for any type of response.

Chapter 31

Dante

My skin feels like it's on fire while Max is bitching at me through the phone. I look down at Demi; she's staring at her fumbling hands. I want to talk to her, reassure her, but I don't even know what I'm thinking. The one girl I've ever loved in my whole life has a child with a douche bag. My heart is tightening like a vice is clamped onto it and my whole chest is weighted down like I'm being buried with rocks, one after another. It's refusing to let up.

"I need your ass down here ASAP!" Max shouts before hanging up. I keep the phone glued to my ear and my movements are rigid as I try to sort through my head. Jameson stole what was mine. That baby should belong to me.

I roll down the partition slightly and raise my voice. "Go to the club." I need to deal with this fire before I can give Demi the attention she deserves. She flinches at the sudden steel in my voice. I open my mouth to say something, but what is there to say?

Slowly, I lower my phone, placing it in my pocket. I feel like an idiot with the rant I went on about children, all while she was listening and never saying a word.

We pull into the parking lot of the club and I roll down the partition once again. "Take Miss Gallo to my house."

She's refusing to look at me and I hate it. I place my hand on her leg. "We'll talk later," I say with a sigh and watch the back of her head bob.

Opening the door, I step out and adjust my suit. I loved seeing the way Demi's face lit up when she looked around the house. It had me happy and content; the first time in a long time I felt that calm from within, and now I have to deal with this shit show.

I go to the bar, taking off my jacket and rolling up the sleeves of my dress shirt. "Where's Sienna?" I ask Robin, who's behind the counter.

"She never showed up for work today."

I grunt, my lips pursing with annoyance. Sienna has never missed a day of work since she started. Robin knows better than to continue a conversation and pretends to clean glasses.

Max whistles at me like I'm his dog, moving his head toward my office. My fingers curl into each other, my knuckles turning white from the strain. Since he's showed up at my club, there has been nothing but problems.

I walk behind my bar, ignoring my brother to pour myself a whiskey. He walks over, waiting at the counter. I down the shot before I pour two more. I hold it out in a silent cheers. We both look over the room in silence as we take our time finishing our drinks.

"You're not going to like this, but it can't be avoided," Max replies.

"And the blows keep coming," I mumble, pushing off the counter and walking toward my office. When we're alone, I ask, "What's the issue now?"

"She's not coming back." My brother's voice is low, far too quiet for his normal demeanor. My heart sputters out of control as I stare at him, void of expression. My first thought is I'd mess any person up when they hang around me too long. There's nothing about my life that screams kid. Then I realize he's not talking about Demi, he's talking about Sienna.

I narrow my eyes. "How and why would you know Sienna is not coming back?" I add her name to add clarification, just in case I'm wrong.

He taps his fist on the arm of his chair, looking down at it before he looks back up at me. "I'm the one who told her to come here to work, because I knew her family would never dare to check here."

"What the fuck are you talking about?" I've had a hard time following the bouncing ball of what he's talking about. My head is too scrambled over the bomb Demi dropped on me to focus at my best.

"She belongs to a motorcycle club a few cities over. Her father is a long-time member, and they think she killed one of theirs. I helped hide her, without you knowing."

My tongue pokes at my inner cheek as I realize my brother has been pulling the strings without me realizing for…who knows how long? A slow poke at my temple announces the start of a headache.

"Let me guess, she was the one stealing money from me and you found out she was responsible for the IP address you were looking for."

"It goes a little deeper than that, I think. I still have no proof. My guess is that Jameson found out who Sienna was and was blackmailing her, and that's why we saw them together. As for the IP address, Jameson was the drug dealer to the guy who tried to hurt Savio's wife. They were using Sienna for the computer access."

I nod, wishing that, at moments like these I could just stand up, walk out of the door, and say, "I quit."

"Does Savio know any of this? I'm sure he would like to know how this is connected to his wife."

"Not yet. But I can assure him his wife is safe. The only danger to her would be the fire they keep throwing on her family, but that's for another day and time."

"Good chat," I say, rubbing at my temples.

"You're taking this better than I thought you would." He stares at me quizzingly.

I wave my hand for him to leave. "I need some time to process."

Max nods, standing to leave. When I'm alone, I drop my head into my hands. I've never seen a positive, moral role model in my life.

A kid. Demi has come so far without me.

I'd drag her farther down if she stayed.

She deserves so much more in life.

I've always been able to give her monetary and materialistic things, but never what she needs. It's why we never worked. I don't know how to give more. It's time I stepped out of my fantasy world I bubbled us in.

Chapter 32

Demi

My whole body is agitated and I can't stop pacing around Dante's house.

"Miss." I jump at the sudden voice.

"Yes?" One of Dante's men is standing behind me, looking sheepish. I hadn't realized anyone was in here.

"I'm sorry I scared you"—he lifts a cell phone towards me—"but you have a phone call."

My heart flutters, wanting to hear Dante's voice as I take the call. "Hello?"

"Demi, I've been trying to get a hold of you for days!" My mother's frantic voice automatically places me on high alert.

"Mom? What's wrong?"

"Oakleigh just kept getting sicker and sicker. I had no way of getting a hold of you, I didn't know what to do." My heart races a mile a minute.

"Where is Oakleigh right now?" I look toward the front door, then around the room. No one is in here anymore. The man left to give me privacy.

"At the hospital, the one with her regular doctor."

"I'm on my way there, sit tight." I hang up the phone, dropping it on the counter before I jog out of the house. I see one man having a smoke off in the distance. I try to walk casually toward his car, and peer in. The keys are in the ignition and the man's back is to me.

I slip into the driver's side door and press the gas down to get to my daughter as fast as I can. My mind is solely focused on getting to the hospital. I never should have left Oakleigh with my mother. I could have made it work. We've *always* just made it work.

The light is red but no one is around, so I slow but don't stop. The next light turns yellow, and I gun the gas to make it through the intersection before it turns red. The parking lot is full at the hospital, like normal. There isn't a single spot near the front entrance so I make my way around the building toward the outskirts before I see a spot.

Jumping out of the car, I turn right into a solid chest. I didn't even see another person. Strong arms hold on to me and I look up into Jameson's eyes.

"And your mother told me you'd never come running, but here you are." The cords on his neck stand out, his entire being strained, and he vibrates with anger.

"What do you want, Jameson?" I hesitantly ask. My eyes dart around the area, as I realize no one knows where I am.

"I want my family back," he sneers, gripping on to me harder. *We were never a family.*

My gut drops and my eyes frantically search the packed lot for anyone to help me. His fingers pinch into my arms and I'm forced to come closer. "We never were a family." I hold myself up strong, refusing to cower to him.

"When Tex called me about you selling yourself, I thought, good girl. You should have lasted a week, tops, and I was supposed to come in and save you."

"Where's my mom?" I ask, not wanting to bring up Oakleigh, hoping he'll get sidetracked.

"That dumb bitch," he scoffs, licking my cheek. I try not to cringe but I can't help it. The wet sliminess has me pulling away. "She thought she could hide my daughter from me. I have to give the old bag credit; she definitely loves her granddaughter more than you."

"Where are they?" I ask again.

"I hooked your mother up with some mind-numbing drugs. She was always the weak one. She's probably sleeping in her bed or trying to get her next score. Did you know why she slept for so many hours back in the day? I'd come in and give her drugs. The drugs helped her stop remembering the shitty hand she's been dealt. But you ran off and she got clean. It was then that I decided to find you."

My stomach twists and my lips feel too heavy to pull up into a fake smile. Each of my muscles tense and I'm going to snap any moment. "Oakleigh. Where is she?" My teeth grind as I speak.

Jameson looks down and crushes his lips to mine. His hand holds the back of my head, my arms flail around trying to get away from his touch. "You always tasted better when you put up a fight." He wipes his mouth with the back of his hand. "Did you think I wouldn't know that she was his?" he sneers.

"She's your daughter, Jameson." My heart pounds so heavily, I worry it might combust. I never feared Jameson physically hurting Oakleigh because she was his blood.

"Bullshit!" he yells into my face. "She was born the exact day you were due with *his*. I saw your calendar with a heart bubbled all around the day."

"She was born early, it's why she has bad lungs," I plead as I try to get away from his grasp.

"I'm not fucking stupid," he growls into my face, his spit hitting me in the mouth. "I thought you would grow to love me. We could be the doting parents we always wanted to be. But you ruined it all. It's what you do. You're a fungus that destroys everything in its path."

"I left you because you're psychotic!" I yell, unable to rein in my temper. His eyes flare and I know it was a bad idea. He opens the van door, tossing me inside. My face hits the floor and my legs hang out, only half on the seat. "Be good. Otherwise, all I have to do is make one phone call, and your daughter is dead."

I want to scream that she is his, but I know better. I've dealt with Jameson when he goes off like this. He's not even close to the same person. I pull myself up and buckle in. My cheek throbs where I hit it when I was tossed in. I rub at the sore spot but stop when I see Jameson watching me through the rear-view mirror.

Chapter 33

Dante

I WALK INTO MY house and pull the tie from around my neck. My thumb slides over the silk and all I can think about is Demi being tied up for my indulgence. She would look so fucking beautiful. My cock twitches, liking the idea all too much.

"Demi," I call out, placing the tie in the back of my dress pants to use later. I'm met with silence. "Where are you, babe?"

I go to the fridge, take out a bottle of beer and a bottle of wine. Using my old party trick, I pop the lid off my beer with my teeth before I pour her a glass of wine.

"Should I pour you a hot bath?" I ask, heading toward my room. I already know I didn't handle our conversation very well earlier. It caught me off guard and I didn't process it well.

The room is empty.

I walk around my house, trying to figure out where she would happily ignore me, but she's nowhere to be seen. The drinks are an annoyance in my hands and I place them down, continuing my search. Each room is empty.

My hands shake as I pull my phone out of my pocket. "Where is Demi?" I ask my security.

"At home."

My mouth dries and it's hard to swallow. "She's not here." The twisted part is, I know I told her she was free, but her leaving was never an option for me. I said that so she would feel better. Never in a million years did I think she would disappear on me. My chest clenches at the thought. "Pull up the surveillance."

I hang up, continuing to search the house, more frantic this time. I go back into our room, thinking it will give more clues. My phone rings as I toss her clothes from the drawers.

"We have her walking out of the house into a black car."

"What car?" I roar.

"The feed cuts out just before. There's no car, then a car is idling, waiting for her to walk to it."

I breathe deeply into my nose. My nostrils flare with each intake. It's then I see the note on the closet door. "I need to think of Oakleigh first, please understand."

I rip the paper off the door, crumpling it into a tiny ball before I toss it to the other side of the room. I thought I finally had what I wanted, which was Demi with me of her own free will and not because I was offering her a better option.

I kick the closet door and it springs off its hinges, falling half haphazardly across the doorway.

"Fuck!" I shout as I turn around in the room.

I may have thought I want Demi of her own free will, but I was wrong. Now that I've had a taste, I will stop at nothing to keep her. She is mine.

My phone rings again. "You better have information," I greet.

"We've located the car. It's at the children's hospital."

I rush to my car, my anger vanishing, replaced with worry. I hate the way it claws into me, its grip unnerving. If I had handled today better, I would have been her first call. Instead, I made her believe she couldn't rely on me. In direct opposition to everything I have ever done for her.

My foot pushes harder on the gas, as I weave in and out of traffic. My GPS directs me to the location of her car, and just my luck there's an open space beside it. I pull in, cutting off the engine, as I jump out of the car. I don't even bother taking my keys with me.

I rush into the hospital, determined to find her. "Her doctor is on the third floor." My earpiece says as I rush toward the elevator. Each floor number lights up at a snail's pace. I could have run up the stairs faster.

"Room 315," I'm directed by my men. The elevator opens. "Turn right." I do as I'm told, walking through the quiet hallways. "Left." Ahead is a desk with a few nurses behind it. I ignore them, not that they call after me. On my right, I see the room and walk in like I own the place.

Three sets of eyes blink at me in shock. "Where is Demi Gallo?" My jaw ticks as I wait for the answer.

"Who?" the doctor asks.

"Demi Gallo and her daughter. Oakleigh is under your care." I hate that I have to explain myself. I make a mental note to find Demi a better doctor who cares about his patients.

His eyes light with familiarity at their names now. "I haven't seen either of them in about a year. They missed their last appointment with me. Now, can you please leave so I can finish up with patients that *do* come to their appointments."

For the first time, my eyes move toward the mother and daughter in the room. There's no point in wasting time to teach this man manners. Demi isn't here, she needs to come first. There's no way she'll ever return to this doctor. I'll find the best doctor in the country.

I turn and slam the door closed. A nearby nurse jumps at the sudden noise that echoes in the hall.

"She's not here," I say to my men, who are listening through my Bluetooth.

I walk out of the hospital with purpose, but it's all for show. My heart cracks more with each step. I think back to all our conversations and find one common topic in each one: she wants to make it on her own. This is her doing that. She took her daughter and left at the first opportunity.

My heart sputters, it's like a knife has been jammed into it and it's trying to work but slowly it's dying…

It won't be long until I'm dead inside once again.

Chapter 34

Demi

Jameson drives us back to my old home before opening the van door and pointing a gun at me. "Time to reunite our happy family," he sneers.

He walks into my mother's house and Oakleigh comes and gives me a big hug. "I missed you so much, mommy!" she declares.

I kiss the top of her head, holding her tight. "I missed you more. Where's Grandma?"

"Sleeping, upstairs."

My eyes glance at the dark stairs that lead to the small hallway up there. "Why don't you go watch some TV, while Jameson and I talk."

"Okay." She walks to the side room where the TV is.

"Hello, Demi." I look up, seeing a large man round the corner from the kitchen. It's the same man from the auction and the fundraiser, Capella.

"That's right, you two know each other. No introductions are needed," Jameson drawls. "I've decided to keep our daughter. You, on the other hand, have been a very naughty girl, and bad girls get punished."

"Dante won't let you get away with this," I declare.

Both men laugh, then the large man pulls my hair and I stumble into him. He pulls his phone out and takes a picture.

"A picture is worth a thousand words. It's time that Dante learns his place."

Dante

I walk around the car Demi left my house in. *Was it all an attempt to make it harder for me to follow her?* I shake my head. *This is a good thing.* She'll do great things without me. The pit of my stomach refuses to allow me to believe she would run away without a word. It's happened before…but even back then she had a valid reason. What is her reason now?

I get back into my car, heading back home. She doesn't even have a cell phone to track.

I call Max through my Bluetooth. "Can you get surveillance on the children's hospital? And get me a location on Demi."

Max chuckles, the sound grating in my ears. "What is it with us Mancini men that makes it almost impossible to hold on to our women?"

A traffic light turns yellow and I gun my car through it, the light turning red as I'm passing through. I don't want to stop until I get home.

"Is that a yes or a no?" I ask, feeling defeated.

"I'll get on it."

I press end, turning up the music until its bass is vibrating through my entire body. When I stop, I'm in my driveway, not remembering the drive back.

My phone buzzes in my pocket, but I ignore it. Instead of going inside, I round the side of the house and go into the backyard. I never come out here except for fight parties.

My phone buzzes again. I pull it out and contemplate tossing it in the pool. I now get the allure of going off the grid like Max and getting away from everything.

My phone goes off again, Max is calling for the third time and a text message from a number I don't recognize. I click on it, and am met with Demi's scared face staring into the camera.

Demi

"Jameson, you're going to regret this," I hiss, not wanting to raise my voice, scared Oakleigh will come and see what's happening. I need to keep her as far away from this as possible.

"No, I'm not." He leans in. "The best part is that I got to have fifty percent of what Dante paid for you, and I get the entire amount from this guy. Must say, you're the best investment I've ever had."

He steps back. "She's all yours."

The two men shake hands while my hair is pulled tight around the auction guy's hand. He doesn't have to tell me to walk. When he moves, so do I. Oakleigh is the only thing on my mind.

He opens his large, cubed van back door. "Get in the cage."

I hesitate and he pushes me forward, my hands catching on the vehicle. Getting on my hands and knees, I crawl into the animal cage. He smiles, locking it, leaving me with no room to stretch out. The hard ground pinches on my skin and knees as I try to move around.

My muscles scream in protest under the strain of the long drive. Hours must have passed by the time the van stops moving. Doors open, and he unlocks the cage.

"Get out." He doesn't have to tell me twice. I crawl out, trying to stretch out my cramped legs. A building stands in front, its roof falling in on sections.

"Soon, this will feel like a castle to you," he pushes me forward. As we enter the house, tall bird-like cages are all around the room with women in them. "This is the next batch of girls I'm selling. I'm going to have you help me train them."

Over my dead body.

"Anything you would like," I reply sweetly, buying me time to come up with a plan. These girls deserve their second chance.

"I'm a little disappointed, Jameson told me you'd be a headache." He grabs my wrists and wraps his belt around them, snugging them tight behind my back.

"Let her go, Capella!" Dante walks in with his two brothers, Romeo, and Savio. They look furious and dangerous.

"Not in this lifetime!" Capella shouts, shooting his gun while pulling me in front of him to act as a human shield. The Mancini men don't return fire, but keep their guns trained on us.

"My daughter is at my mother's house with Jameson, save her and forget about me!" I cry, tears pouring down my cheeks as I realize I didn't even get to hug my daughter goodbye. It could have been the last time I ever saw her.

Dante steps closer, ignoring my words. "Dante!" I plead for him to do as I say.

Capella fires again, skimming Dante in the arm. My heart is hammering out of my chest as I slam my foot down on the man holding me and try to pull away. I hear three shots, and Capella falls to the ground.

Dante comes running toward me, lifting me in his arms. "Are you okay?" His hands run down and over my body, searching for any sign of a wound.

"We have to get Oakleigh!" I frantically yell, on the verge of a panic attack.

"We have her, babe. It took Max five minutes alone with Jameson to have him crying like a little girl, and for him to tell us everything we needed to find you."

"What do you mean? You have her?" I ask, pulling away.

"She's with Max, safe and around the block. I didn't want her to see the shit show in here." His words are a blur as I run out to see my daughter. I hear him talking in his commanding voice, to me or someone else, I don't know as I push ahead, needing to know Oakleigh is safe.

I step outside, seeing a car come to a stop. Oakleigh gets out of the black sedan and comes barreling at me. We collide with a thud and I hold her as tight as I can. "I love you so much! Are you okay?" I ask.

"I'm...fine...mom. Max and his brothers...got me." Her words are split between coughs as she begins one of her coughing spells. All I can do is rub her back.

"When was the last time you took medication?" I ask her, even though she can't respond yet. On the outside, I'm trying to be patient, but on the inside I'm reeling.

"This morning. Grandma gives it to me every day..." She finally says when she has her coughing under control.

"Really?" I ask, shocked.

"Yeah. She's really nice too. It's not the same without you, but we have fun together. She even set me up in a school and I have two friends!"

I'm stunned we're talking about the same mother I grew up with. The woman she's describing is a past memory I hardly remember.

"You girls are safe now," Dante tells us as he approaches.

"Thank you, Dante!" Once again, this man has saved me.

"As a precaution, I'm having my doctor check you both." He kneels to Oakleigh's height. "I'm Dante, I didn't have time to introduce myself to you earlier." He extends his hand and she takes it. Oakleigh has never been very trusting. They shake hands and she gives him one of her megawatt smiles that always melts my heart.

"Do you mind if I talk to your mom for a second?"

She shakes her head no and he places his hand on my lower back to lead me a few feet away. "Are you okay? Physically, you look alright, but I don't know how else to help you right now."

Why the hell does he always have to be so damn sweet. "I'll be okay. I'm still processing," I answer truthfully.

"You have a great girl on your hands. I can see why you talk so passionately about her and children in general. I never understood it, until now, I think."

He's pulling on my heartstrings. I can't stand the lie anymore. I can't stand the way he thinks I'm this perfect person when I'm the villain and have been since the moment I walked into his club.

I swallow, knowing what has to be said. "I was pregnant with twins, but I didn't know that at the time. After I left the hospital, I began to bleed and I miscarried one of them. It was so early in the pregnancy; I never questioned it, but then I found out I was still pregnant with one. She's yours Dante, I swear I've never touched Jameson, but I had to tell him that Oakleigh was his so he wouldn't hurt her."

The memory of that day flashes before me like it was today.

I'm pushed up against a wall, my head bounces off the flat surface. Jameson grips my chin as hard as he can, while I'm disorientated. "What did you say?" he snarls before hitting my head against the wall again.

"I'm pregnant with your baby," I cry.

His lips curl downwards. "You refuse to fuck me, Demi. You've only ever been Dante's slut."

"It's never been like that." The lie tastes like acid on my tongue. God, I wish I knew where Dante went. I miss him so much and I'm lost without him. My hand wants to rub at my small, protruding bump. I

write letters to my unborn child each night and tell her all the good things in my life. It mostly consists of things about her and Dante.

"Don't you remember? It was months ago, when you barged in here, and I took care of you."

"That's right, I remember now, I fucked you really good."

I nod up and down, hoping he'll release me.

"You owe me for my sperm." *He releases me and I run to my purse. It's my last hundred-dollar bill. I pull it out, giving it to him.*

"Now thank me."

"Thank you, Jameson."

My eyes blur and Dante is fuzzy when I look back at him.

He stands there staring at me as my tears fall over my lashes as the pain of finally telling the truth washes through me. The truth I couldn't even repeat to myself because I was too scared. Scared of what Jameson would do. Scared that I would never see Dante again to tell him about his daughter.

Dante looks stumped. He glances over at Oakleigh, then to me. "I'm her father?" he questions, taking a step back from me. "Why would Jameson think she's his? I knew I should have killed the bastard years ago."

"While I was pregnant, I thought Jameson was going to kill me and our baby, the lie just...slipped out. I told him it happened on a night that he was too drunk to remember."

He tilts his head, his posture stiff, and I can see the invisible walls he holds sliding into place. I watch as his jaw ticks back and forth.

"I looked for you, and tried to find where you went. I got so desperate I even asked your mother."

Dante is silent. He tilts his chin up, and swallows hard. A harsh scoff leaves his throat as he gives me a slow, disbelieving head shake. I'm forced to watch his once-clear eyes turn slightly pink as he looks away from me. His expression burns into my memory, scalding deep within.

He nods to someone behind me and Max is suddenly there, grasping hold of my arm.

"I'm not going anywhere with Max or without my daughter." I jerk my arm but it stays firmly in his brother's grasp.

Dante steps into my space, grabbing me by both arms, and I go limp in his hold.

"I'm getting Oakleigh checked over then I'll drop her off and deal with you."

Dante tugs on me and my body jerks forward, my chest slamming into his.

My agony shreds everything in me. "What's there to deal with?"

"I'm fucking lost for words right now, Dem. I wish I knew this information earlier so I could have dealt with Jameson myself. And then there's the fact that I'm a father. My brain is short circuiting with all of this information," he seethes, allowing for his words to linger. "I'm going to do a paternity test and if you are lying, no one will ever see you again."

"I promise, I'm not lying. I had to protect her, and the only way I could protect her from Jameson was to tell him she was his."

His fingers slowly release their hold on me. "Max will take you to Margaret's house." He turns his back to me and I watch him crouch down to talk to Oakleigh. I can't hear what he's saying. I use my palms to wipe my eyes, not wanting her to see me in such a state.

She peers over at me. "Are you coming, Mom?" she asks.

I suck in my lips, shaking my head, forcing my tears to stop. I could yell, but what's the point? It would scare her and I know she's safe. That's all I have ever wanted for her.

"No, Honey. I need to make sure everyone is safe here, but I'll see you soon."

She comes running at me, hugging my torso. "I love you, Mom." I don't deserve a daughter so fantastic.

I sniffle, kissing her head. "I love you more. Dante is a good man. He's going to make sure you're safe until I'm with you."

I watch as she gets into the back of Dante's car and he slides in after her. The black sedan rolls down the street and I watch it until it disappears out of my view.

"Come on, let's go." Max opens the passenger door and waits for me to move.

"What about the girls inside?" I nibble on my lip, not wanting to leave until they are safe too. As if on cue, three vehicles pull up.

"Those are Dante's paramedics. They'll check them over and give them a safe place to sleep."

"Who makes sure they're safe?"

"Listen, Demi, that's a conversation for you and Dante. My job is to take you to Margaret's house. We can do this the easy way or the hard way, it's up to you."

Reluctantly, I slip into the car, watching the men from the cars go into the house with what looks like medical bags slung over their chests.

Max gets into the driver's seat. No fancy drivers for him, I guess.

"Dante said you made Jameson cry." Just saying his name aloud has my chest squeezing.

Max looks at me with an evil grin that stretches across his face. "Don't worry, you daughter saw nothing. Dante made sure of it."

"Is he still alive?"

"A gentleman never kills and tells." He winks. "But I can assure you, he will never harm you or your daughter again." Immediately, my chest releases and I'm able to take a calming breath.

"Thank you," I say quietly, looking out the window.

"Trust me, the pleasure was all mine."

Chapter 35

Dante

I'M SITTING BESIDE MY *daughter.*

The word daughter feels foreign.

I'm searching for any resemblance to me, but all I can see is Demi.

"Why do you keep looking at me strangely?" Oakleigh asks innocently.

"I'm not trying to. I just can't believe how much you look like your mother. Has anyone ever said you look like your dad?"

Her lips twist and she glances at me strangely. "Most kids like me don't have dads."

"Like you?"

She sighs, like she can't believe she has to explain something to a person like me. "I've only ever lived with my mom, and there have been times where we lived in the back seat of her car. We're always moving. I never had time for a dad."

I want to desperately ask who she thinks her dad is, but I'm too scared of how she might react. If she starts crying on me, I'll have no idea what to do and I don't want to screw this up.

I want to believe Demi but I can't until I have physical proof. She has spent the last ten years having Jameson believe Oakleigh was his. What if she's not mine or Jameson's?

We pull up to my home and Oakleigh's face is smushed up against the glass.

"You live here?" she asks excitedly.

"I do. The doctor is already waiting. He's going to take some blood and listen to your chest and back for that cough you have."

She opens the door, looking around, but each step is cautious. "Is Mom meeting us here? Why was she crying? Am I a bad daughter because I didn't wait for her?" She breaks my heart with her questions.

"Your mother's priority is you, Oakleigh, she wanted you to get checked out. Demi has always told me what a good person you are and how sweet and kind you are. You will never be a bad daughter."

I open the front door and my doctor has set up a mini exam room in the front living area. I wanted the space to be open to make sure Oakleigh wouldn't be frightened.

My phone buzzes and it's a text message from Max. **Demi is at the house. I'll stay outside on watch.**

"Hi, Oakleigh," my doctor greets. Everything takes about a half hour, but man, Oakleigh can talk. She never stopped unless she had a coughing fit, and as soon as we asked about her condition, I don't think she took a breath.

"Do I get a candy now that I'm done? It's what I normally get." My doctor looks at me as if to say I *don't keep candy.*

"I think I have some ice cream in the freezer you can have." That satisfies her question.

We both walk him to the door and I open it to find Sienna standing there. The doctor slips between the door and her, seeing himself out. Her presence takes me a second to recover from just standing there, shocked.

"Oakleigh, why don't you go to the kitchen to see if you can find that ice cream?"

She looks at Sienna then me. "If you want me to leave you two alone, all you have to do is ask."

I open my mouth to respond but she taps my arm and walks away.

I look back at the one person I considered my best friend. "Didn't think I'd see you again." I cross my arms, not moving from my spot.

"Don't look at me like I just ran over your puppy."

I narrow my eyes. "Why are you here? Max told me you showed up at Throne of Sin because he told you to. I'm sure he would like to know you're here bothering me."

"Stop being a drama queen. You're still my best friend." She twists her toes in semicircles, a sign she has to ask for something she doesn't want to. "But I need to find Max. Do you know where he is?"

I shake my head at how my day has turned out. "I'll drive you there."

For the first time in my life, I wish I wasn't the nice guy, but it goes against my DNA to be anything else.

Leaning into the house, I call, "Oakleigh, change of plans. We'll get ice cream along the way and then go see your mom!"

She comes skipping toward me a second later.

"Should I ask?" Sienna whispers, looking at me then her.

"Nope. Just get into the car."

We pull up to the house and Sienna steps out, followed by Oakleigh. I stay behind for a second, not knowing what the hell I'm doing. Oakleigh bends back into the car, giving me a smile. "The proper thing to do is walk me to the door," she directs.

I think I may have already lost my heart to this girl, daughter or not.

Oakleigh stands there, licking her ice cream as she waits for me. Not a single drop has landed on the side of the cone or her hand.

I stretch my legs out the door, cramped from riding in the back seat, and stand, unable to face Demi yet. "I'll watch you from here, but you'll see me tomorrow when I come by." I try to give her what I think is an encouraging smile.

She skips off but only makes it a few yards before skipping back. "Thanks for the ride!"

I watch until Demi opens her door, then slip back into the car. My phone buzzes, it's the lab results. Opening it up, I glance away. Maybe it's better to never know. My eyes glance down, skimming through. My hand shakes the entire time, making it really fucking hard to keep my place in this jumble of medical jargon. In the middle, I see the ninety-nine point nine percent chance that Oakleigh is mine. It's big and bold, staring back at me. My muscles forget how to work and I fall back into the seat, my phone falling, forgotten, to the floor.

I have a kid. My hand runs down my face, pulling at my skin. *Fuck me.* I feel like I've been run over by a truck and it keeps reversing and going forward over my chest. I wipe at my itchy eyes, and they feel so much better being closed. I don't know the first damn thing to do, and I pride myself with always feeling in control. *Oakleigh is my daughter.* The thought consumes me.

I've heard men joke about having children out there, but I've rolled my eyes, knowing this was never a possibility for me. Here I am now, and this is no joke. My body jolts and I punch the seat in front of me.

I'm a father. The reality slams into my chest, taking my breath away. I could have been giving that little girl everything I had to help make her life happy, safe, and healthy. Instead, my daughter had to endure poverty and illness.

My neck burns and it creeps into my cheeks as my anger builds from deep within. "Take me to a children's store," I demand, with the partition down a crack.

I reach over to the side of the sedan and pull out the bottle of whiskey. I take a swig of the liquid, not caring about a glass. Growing up, we used to talk about how getting a girl pregnant was a death sentence, but I'm not nineteen years old anymore. I'm a man, who takes care of his own. I have to be. My fist jets out once again to punch the seat in front of me.

I take another swig of whiskey but it doesn't even burn going down. Instead, it's smooth and full-bodied. What I need is the cheap stuff I used to drink as a teen. That stuff would put hair on anyone's chest.

"Change of plans, liquor store first."

I wake with my head pounding. Everything hurts, starting at my temple down to my legs. I sit up, using my hand to push on the hard floor. It takes a few tries to open my eyes enough to realize I don't know where the fuck I am.

Beside me is an Advil and a glass of water. I pick up the small pill, looking at the black lettering. The pounding refuses to stop. Each muscle protests as I pop the pill and take a gulp of the room temperature water.

I look back down and realize my head was resting on a medium-sized tie-dyed bunny. I grab it, its soft fur melting into my strong grasp.

My knees crack as I drag myself into a standing position.

"Good morning!" Oakleigh is staring at me, bright eyed and happy.

I clear my throat. "Morning." I look around at the room but nothing indicates this is a nine-year-old's room. It smells like an old person.

"Thank you for the rabbit." She tilts her head toward my hands.

"Ah, yes. Here you go." My voice is gruff and cracks as I wake up.

She giggles. I have no idea what I said that was funny. "So, you're my dad, huh?" she questions.

I'm way too tired and hungover to be having this conversation.

"Mom told me last night. It's okay, I just found out too. The only thing to do from here is get to know each other. Mom said you two grew up together and lived across the street from each other."

She's looking at me expectantly.

"Where is Demi?" I ask, rubbing at the side of my head.

"Oak, why don't you go outside while Dante and I have a chat."

I stare at Demi and what keeps running through my mind is that Oakleigh looks exactly like her.

"I want to get to know my daughter," I say stiffly.

She nods. "I'm sorry for how all this went down, Dante. I wish I could change the past for you—so you could have found out about her sooner. It will always be my regret."

"You and me both." I sigh. "My car will come and get her tomorrow and then drop her back off. I'll pay for this house, since Oakleigh will be staying here."

I stare into her gorgeous face. It's as emotionless as mine, and her eyes...they look as dead as my soul. *Good*. I'm petty like that. I want her to hurt so bad that she sinks into herself. Every time she looks into the mirror, I want her to remember the pain she has caused.

"What about us?" she questions softly.

"I don't know Dem, I'm still processing that I'm a father."

I hand her a cell phone. "This is for Oakleigh. I want her to call me any time she wants."

She takes it, placing it on the counter behind her. "I love you Dante."

I ignore her sad voice. "Oakleigh and I will spend the day together tomorrow. Like I said, I'll send my driver for her. Now excuse me, I'm going to say goodbye to my daughter and let her know." Demi nods, her eyes puffy and red.

I march out of her house, looking for my daughter.

Chapter 36

Demi

THE NEXT DAY, I insist I go with Oakleigh to Dante's. She looks so brave walking up to his house alone. He opens the door, gives her a hug, then glares at me through the blacked-out car window until we start rolling away.

The partition has stayed down the entire time. "Can you drive me to my mother's?"

"Yes, ma'am." No need to give him her address, he goes there without asking any questions.

The car stops at the base of the driveway and the first thing I see is my old car. "Thank you," I mumble, stepping out. I walk around my car in disbelief. I never thought I'd see it again. It looks like it was just washed and I wonder if my mother saw who dropped it off.

I knock three times at the front door and get no answer. My hand reaches above the porch light that has never worked and slips a key off the dirty top.

"Mom!" I holler. My stomach rolls with nausea, scared of not knowing what I'll find. *Time to wear my grownup panties.* Maybe she's not home, or she's just sleeping.

We've never been close, but she is my mother and I still love her. She did the best she could, and she did good by my daughter.

My steps creek along the stairs as I go toward my mother's room and push her door open with my finger to find her in bed. I hold her hand, it's colder than mine. Placing my two fingers on her neck, I search for her pulse. I can't find it. My hands shake uncontrollably as I take the phone Dante gave me and call 9-1-1.

The ambulance comes within minutes, which is strange for this part of town. Instead of taking us to the small hospital with limited resources, we are taken into the city to the bigger hospital. I can't help but wonder if this is all because of Dante, but how would he know? I have to stop thinking about him. An image of his dark eyes, hooded, staring me down, flashes before my eyes and I shake my head to have it disappear.

He's done with me, as he should be.

It would hurt less if I felt he wasn't right. I deserve the punishment. I deserve everything I get. An hour later, at the hospital, my mother is declared dead. She was still alive when I found her. If I arrived earlier, I could have saved her.

Dante's driver is by the emergency exit when I leave the building. I would love to keep walking and refuse the ride, but I don't even have money for an Uber right now.

"Thank you for picking me up. Can you take me to my mother's house, please?" I greet, opening the door and taking a seat inside. The entire way, I close my eyes with my head leaned back, allowing the sway of the car to loll me back and forth. The jerking motion of stopping wakes me from my light sleep and I look through the window to find I'm right where I started, back in my old neighborhood.

"Thank you," I say as I step out.

I walk into my old home, into the kitchen, and open the fridge door. It's empty except for milk. I open the cupboard and see a box of cheerios and a bag of jellybeans. The jellybeans call to me. I open the bag, pouring myself a handful. My mouth waters, and I already know the moment I have one, I'll end up eating it all, until my stomach hurts. My hand is midair, ready to pour a handful into my mouth, when I spot a prescription bottle staring at me in the corner. It'll be easier to numb the pain than to process it.

I place the candy on the counter, grabbing the orange plastic jar. My hand pushes down and twists the lid open, sliding two pills out from the bottle. I easily toss them in my mouth, before realizing I cannot be my mother.

I run to the sink, spitting them out. I take the candy on the counter, tossing them in the garbage and the bag next to them. If I get hungry, I'll eat the cereal.

It's not even noon and I'm exhausted. The comfort of my old room calls to me.

It feels strange to sleep in my old bed knowing that Dante isn't on the other side of the street. Each time I turn in bed, the clock has moved twenty minutes. My eyes feel heavier than they did before I tried to nap, but I drag my tired and sore body out of bed and into the shower.

Cold water rains down on me, and I hit the wall with my palm, hoping to jiggle it into warmth. It does nothing. Within seconds, I'm as clean as I can be. There's a ratty old towel hanging up and it gives me the shivers just looking at it. I decide to air dry, before I place the same clothes back on.

How is the day going? I text Dante. I probably should have texted sooner, but I'm not used to having a phone.

No response.

I sit on my mother's bed staring at my cell, willing for it to ping. A half hour later, I lay down, hugging my knees as I stare at the black screen. Eventually I fall asleep even though it's still early in the day.

The sound of a garbage truck wakes me up and it's already late in the afternoon. Still no response from Dante.

My keys are nowhere to be found, so I have no way to go to Dante's to make sure everything is okay. I just need to trust in him. It's not an easy concept for me. My go-to defense mechanism is to avoid, so I start cleaning out my mother's room, boxing up her clothes, as I create my mental checklist on what needs to be done, and what bills need to be paid.

"Sorry to hear about your mother," I jump, my hand flying to my chest. Turning, Dante is leaning against the door frame, looking like a dangerous God reigning above his people.

"You're just jealous," I deflect, not wanting to accept the reality that she's gone yet, while knowing he would love to bury his own mother. I'm scared once the reality of her death hits, I'll spiral, and I can't afford to do that right now.

"You have a way with luck." He pushes off the frame and walks toward me. "Oakleigh is downstairs petting the cat. Let me take you girls home."

I place my hand on his chest. Feeling the zing of our chemistry immediately, I withdraw it just as quickly. "We're staying here."

His jaw works itself over and back. "It's not safe here. I won't allow my daughter to be in danger."

"I can't be relying on you for everything, Dante. You can't always be the protector."

His eyes grow large, his jawline sharper than ever. "There's a difference between being stubbornly stupid and keeping our daughter safe."

I flinch over his harsh words. "I've been keeping her safe her entire life. You just entered the picture." As soon as the words are out of my mouth, I regret them.

Dante walks toward me and I step back until my back hits the closet door. "And whose fault is that?" He questions in a low, growly voice.

I straighten my back, refusing to cower. "I had no idea where you went and was young and scared. I did the best I could."

"Bullshit. You found me the moment you decided you needed something from me again."

"Not true. I had no idea you owned Throne of Sin and the moment I found out, I walked out, looking for another way."

"That was your first mistake. You should have told me then."

The pit in my stomach twists, squeezing my insides. "I know okay!"

"Now, you're getting into my car even if I have to toss you over my shoulder and tie you down."

"You wouldn't dare. Not with Oakleigh."

"Try me." His eyes glow with an animalistic, wild haze. He's determined to get his way, no matter what.

I stare up at his hardened features. "I want a list of what's not safe with this house. Once it's fixed, you cannot stop me from staying here."

He dips his face down to my level and his lips touch my earlobe. "You're in no position to be placing demands on me. I'm holding on by a thread, trying not to lose my temper with you. Now, be a good girl and get in the fucking car."

His baritone voice vibrates down to my core. I shove past him, my shoulder stinging from the force of impact. I hear his steps behind me as he trails me back to the main floor.

"Oakleigh!" I call, not seeing her. My heart rate spikes before I see her outside trying to wrangle the cat into her arms. I open the screen door. "Time to go, hun."

"Can Stitch come?"

"Of course," Dante says from behind me and it has me stewing. She was asking me.

He takes one look at my face and must know. "Relax, you will always be her number one. All I'm asking is to get to know my daughter."

It seems like so much more than that, and I'm so scared of losing her, because of my mistake.

Chapter 37

Dante

I HAVE A DAUGHTER who is smart, kind, and beautiful. It's hard to wrap my mind around. I say the words out loud, but I don't believe them. I don't know how to be a dad.

I fold the page edge over, marking my spot in my parenting for dummies book, before looking over at the five other books on my counter. My eyes are dry and tired as I rub at them before checking my phone to watch Demi and our daughter eating dinner together at Margaret's. Right now, my men are placing cameras throughout her mother's house, changing the locks, and putting an alarm system in. Demi is stubborn as Hell, and will only stay where I tell her for so long. I'm shocked she even agreed to the two nights away from her childhood home.

Part of me is excited to see her react to the upgraded security I've added without her consent. She doesn't get it. I'll do anything to keep them safe. They're my family. Nothing more needs to be said.

The next day, Demi and Oakleigh arrive at my house on time with my driver. I open the door of the car and take a seat in the back.

The space is tight and my leg brushes against Demi's. She tries to move over, but it's not far enough for us not to touch.

"Stop being dramatic," I whisper so that only she can hear.

Her lips purse into a scowl that looks all too cute on her.

My driver already knows the plan and heads back to our old neighborhood. I can tell Demi wants to ask questions but refuses. We stop at the end of her old driveway, the one I used to keep watch over.

"Here are your new keys." I place one of them into Oakleigh's hands and drop the other into Demi's lap when her hand doesn't come up. "Your set also has the car keys on it."

I open the door, closing it after me, but jog to the other side, opening Oakleigh's for her.

"I've changed the locks and added an alarm system."

"I'm going to go to the backyard and let you two talk," Oakleigh says, walking away.

"Now you've made her uncomfortable," Demi chastises.

"You have made it perfectly clear that you want nothing from me. But you will not stop me from ensuring the safety of our daughter." I give her a tight smile that riles her up more. The more we argue, the more relaxed and comfortable I become. This is a part of who we are and it comes so naturally.

"Now, excuse me. I'm taking our daughter shopping for her new bedroom."

Demi pinches her nose, breathing loudly. "Dante! I have this under control. You buy for your house, and I'll buy for mine."

I give her a cocky shrug and walk away, leaving her stomping her feet. "You better go learn the alarm system." I toss over my shoulder and hear her give a small, adorable growl. Making Demi angry is almost as fun as making her happy.

"Hey, Kiddo. Want to go for ice cream while your mother works on the house?"

"Did you know if you have a dog your house is thirty-five percent less likely to be broken into?"

I think about her comment and ask, "Would you feel safer if we got you a puppy?"

Her entire face lights up, and I already know we're coming back with any animal she wants. "Go say bye to your mom and let's go look." She smiles, running off, and is back before I even have a hand on the door handle.

"Do you want to look at some breeder websites for dogs?" I already have one pulled up the moment we drive away.

"No, most of those can be puppy mills. I want to get one from the shelter and be the one to give it a second chance."

"I know just the place." When I was twelve, I had to do a community service job for vandalism and it happened to be at the local Humane Society.

The moment we walk in, I'm easily recognized. It's the same nice old woman who ran the place twenty years ago and she has short curly gray hair, still looking like she's a hundred years old. I wonder what her real age is...

"Dante!" She slowly walks over and takes one of my hands in both of hers. "It's nice to see you again."

"My daughter here would like to adopt a pet."

Her eyes light up and she looks down at Oakleigh. "Wonderful!" She lets go of my hand and starts asking Oakleigh a bunch of questions.

It takes us two hours of playing with every dog or cat in the back room before she decides on a two-year-old golden retriever.

Oakleigh's smiles and laugh are addicting. I find myself smiling and laughing with her.

"Let's go show your mom," I say after I've also purchased a collar, leash, dog bed, food, and some toys Oakleigh picked out. Whatever she asked for, I gave her, because who am I to say no? I have nine years of not being around to make up for.

This is the first time my smile slips as I think about everything I've missed, the time I'll never get back.

The dog, who isn't named yet—Oakleigh wants Demi to help name it—jumps up on my lap and licks me in the face.

"Alright." I laugh, brushing it off and back to Oakleigh.

We get back to the old neighborhood and Oakleigh runs to the front door. I stand there looking around, not understanding why Demi would ever want to come back here. I would love nothing more than to light my old house on fire and here she is trying to make hers a home again.

The door opens before we get to the steps. My arms are overflowing with dog stuff while Oakleigh chases the dog without a name.

"What do we have here?" Demi asks with one of her fake smiles.

"A dog to help protect us!" Oakleigh yells with delight. It's the most perfect sound I've ever heard.

"I can see that. Why don't you take it to the backyard and make sure it pees?"

She runs through the house to the backyard and Demi levels me with a look. "A dog, Dante?"

I walk past her and into the house, placing the dog stuff down before heading into the kitchen to put its food and water dishes down.

"You can't get her everything she asks for."

Ignoring her, I fill the metal dish with cold water and place it on the floor.

"You need to ask me first over stuff like this. I can't afford to feed a dog right now!"

I stand to my full height and stalk toward her. "I can do whatever I want because you hid her from me. For *nine* years. If she asks me for a fucking lion, I'll buy her the whole damn zoo. I will take care of the dog bills. Your job is to love and take care of it, and in return it will protect you," I sneer, my anger wanting to consume me.

"When will you see I need to stand on my own two feet?"

I get right into her personal space. "When you actually try and do something about it!"

She's doing her deep breathing thing again, and her brows pinch together, wrinkling her forehead. "Why have I seen a police car driving past here every hour?"

I shrug. "I have no idea." *Lies.* And it's every forty-five minutes, not every hour. "I'm done with your bullshit for today. I'm going to say goodbye to my daughter and leave. You can make our life easier by not talking to me when I pick her up from now on."

Chapter 38

Demi

A MONTH HAS PASSED and I've tried to avoid Dante as much as possible. In front of Oakleigh, we stay civil, even when it's impossibly hard because Dante is determined to make my life difficult. He goes out of his way to ruin my day if he can.

My phone rings. "Hello?"

"You realize this is not your phone, right? I bought it for Oakleigh, yet she is never the one answering it."

"I'll go get her." I pull the phone away from my ear, not wanting to hear his deep voice.

"Not so fast, Demi."

Reluctantly, I place the phone back to my ear. "What is it?" I ask, annoyed. I already know I'm not going to like whatever he says.

"It's time that Oakleigh starts having sleepovers at my house. We've done it your way for a month. Now I want what real half custody looks like. She needs to start living at my house too."

Instantly, my pulse quickens, my chest vibrates from the sudden thumping of my uncontrolled heartbeats.

"We said in a few months."

"I changed my mind. I have a shed out back you can sleep in if you want to stay close."

I squeeze my eyes shut. I knew this day would come, but I'm struggling with being away from her.

"Do you want to tell her the good news or shall I?" I can hear his smile on the other end. If I smash the phone, he won't be able to contact us, and maybe I could prevent him taking my daughter.

I hang up instead. It's a coward move, when I already know I won't refuse the request.

"Demi, you can't avoid this." Dante's voice echoes in my house.

What the fuck?

"How am I hearing you?" I ask, turning in a circle searching in the small room.

He laughs! Asshole.

"Oakleigh wanted an Alexa, so I bought her four. She placed them all over the house. Now I can talk to her just by saying a simple command."

I spot the small black circular AI machine. "How long have these been in our house?"

"Focus, Demi. Are you telling her or am I?"

I grumble, but part of me loves how much effort he's gone to, to keep her happy. "I'll tell her, but you better not disappoint her."

"The only person I enjoy disappointing is my mother."

With that, I walk out of the house, needing a walk to calm my nerves. In the end, I know it's my fears controlling my views. This is a good thing, and will make Oakleigh happy.

Dante

"Dante, you're a half hour early. Oakleigh is in the shower." Demi's hand stays holding the front door open.

I stand in my usual suit, and notice the moment my regular cologne wafts past her. Her lips lift into a smirk and I bet she has no idea of her reaction. "I wanted to talk to you first," I say.

My head tilts up, motioning that I'd like to talk inside. It takes everything in me not to walk right in. I'm not used to rules when it comes to Demi, but I'm trying here.

Instead, she steps out and closes the door behind her. "What type of conversation?" she asks. "If we go inside, Oakleigh might hear." She sounds nervous. I watch as she crosses her arms and leans against the door before changing her position to her hands by her side. Her hand touches her hair, before placing it on the door knob.

"We need to start bridging this gap between us," I state matter of factly. It comes out forced and direct, the opposite of how I practiced this conversation going.

I watch as surprise flickers across her face.

"I couldn't agree more. I'll be honest with you. I appreciate everything you have done for Oakleigh, even though it's been hard to accept. I would love for it to go back to how we were, but you need to decide if you forgive me for not telling you about Oakleigh. I can see the pain I've caused you, but we'll never get there unless you can get over it."

She sounds like Savio. He almost said the exact thing.

I flex my jaw up and down, and her lips twist. "I'm working on it." My stomach flutters as I try to find the right words. I've never been edgy around Demi before, but this conversation has my nerves wanting to jump out of my skin. "How would you feel about coming out for dinner with us before Oakleigh sleeps over tonight?" I clear my throat, cringing at how my voice sounded.

Oakleigh has been sleeping over one night each week for the last month. Each time I pick up Oakleigh, I can see Demi relaxing a bit more.

"Yeah, I would like that. Thank you." Her posture relaxes and I feel like a weight has been lifted from my shoulders. I want to tell Demi that I've forgiven her, but for some reason I can't force the words out of my mouth yet.

My cheeks strain from the smile that refuses to leave my face, and we stand outside awkwardly like we both want to say more but don't know what to say at the same time.

"Okay then." I nod my head. "Should I wait for you in the car until you girls are ready?" I take a step back, my heart racing.

"Dante, come in. I'll show you a few new tricks Scotia has learned while we wait."

Demi

"Guess what?" I squeal to Oakleigh as I run out to the front yard with the phone still in my hand. "I'm starting to work with a midwife!" I finally found someone who will take me on as I did classes to get my accreditation. The pay is almost nonexistent, leaving me worse off financially than before, but like clockwork, money appears in an envelope, just like Tex said it would.

Oakleigh places the hose down where she's standing and comes to give me a great big hug. "I knew you would do it!"

"Thank you, honey." I pick up the hose she was using to water the half-dead flowers. "Why don't you go play with Scotia and I'll finish up here."

I don't need to say anything more and she's running inside. I have to admit, Scotia is a great dog and I would miss not having her around now that she's been here for a week. Each day, Dante comes and visits with Oakleigh and we're able to talk a little bit more. Once a week, Oakleigh gets to sleep over at his house, which allows me to take any night shifts when the time comes. Until then, I'm hoping to get a job that will help pay the bills.

A door slamming has me looking behind and I see Dante's mom coming out in her nightgown even though it's the afternoon. I've seen her a few times, and each time she's in that mumu.

"Looks like the little whore had to come back home. You're as bad as he is!" she screams at me as she crosses the street. Her feet march onto my front yard as she storms toward me. "You poisoned his brain and made him run away from his mama, and now he's worse than his father. Not even God himself will save my boys and you're to blame." She spits at my feet. I'm too shocked to say anything or move. "The best thing Dante did was leave your sorry ass behind..."

Her tirade continues as I break down on the inside. All I've ever wanted was to be kind and show my love. My thumb moves over the water to increase the pressure and I hold the green hose up to her, spraying her.

"Looks like you need help cooling down."

Mrs. Mancini screams and curses at me before she runs back to her side of the street.

"Come back to bother me again and I'll get my gun and pop your ass."

She makes a cross symbol over her chest and I continue with my watering, even though my hands are shaking uncontrollably. She really is a mean old lady.

"Demi, I can't take Oakleigh tonight," Dante informs me over the phone. We already have our shoes on and are about to wait outside for his car. Oakleigh is nearing the end of her fifteen-minute goodbye skit she does every time we leave Scotia.

I step out and close the door behind me. "No. If we're going to do this, you have to be all in. You can't just decide minutes before that it no longer works with your schedule."

He groans into the phone. "It's not like that. I have business to attend to tonight. It's important."

"No, your daughter is important. I'll take my car and drop her off for you."

"I know she's important, I never said she wasn't!"

"You just did by choosing business over her." I'm vibrating in place. This is unfair to Oakleigh and I was hoping to make some money tonight.

"Fuck," he hisses between what sounds like clenched teeth. "Never mind, tonight is perfect."

It doesn't sound perfect and I waffle on if I should make her go, but I don't want him to be the type of dad that's halfway in. "Good. See you soon."

"I'll have my car come," he argues.

"Too late. We're already in the car and driving." I hang up and get Oakleigh before Dante sends someone.

After dropping Oakleigh off with Dante, I head into Throne of Sin. "Demi!" Robin greets me immediately. "What are you doing here?"

"I heard you guys are short staffed and need some help." By the looks of it, it's true. I was hoping they could use help.

"Dante will have my head if you help."

"He's not here, is he? I'll just work for tips and no one has to know. I can already tell you guys are slammed and can't keep up." On cue, some guy hollers at Robin about needing a drink.

"Fine, but I know nothing about this. I'm innocent." Her hands come up, looking uncertain if she's making the right call.

I give her a hug and quickly go out back to change. There's a new bartender behind the counter that's half the speed of Sienna and I wonder why Sienna's not here as I grab a tray and the bartender tells me the table number for the drinks.

"Here are your drinks gentlemen," I greet a table of men I've never seen around. They all have matching vests. Must be a motorcycle group passing by. I give each man a shot glass of clear liquid and a lime.

One of them stands and says, "Half hour until victory, men!" They all raise their drinks and cheer.

They all ignore me, as I clean up the glasses. A few of the men order more drinks but never look at me. They're too busy talking with each other in hushed voices. It's their tone that gets my attention.

"He'll never see us coming."

"Here, here!"

One of them waves a hundred up into the air and Shelby sashays by right away.

"Do you have time for a quick lap dance, darlin'?" The man with the money asks.

I watch as two of them are led toward the back booths with thick black curtains. It's for the "quick" lap dances. A bunch of college boys are near the back and I go toward them, wanting to keep an eye on these guys. There's something about them.

"What can I get you boys?" I ask in a cheery voice.

"I'd take you on a platter," one of them flirts. I have to fight the eye roll that threatens to make itself known.

"It's your lucky day. I'll give you a quick two-minute dance for free."

I drag him behind the curtain, trying to hear the conversation. Much to my disappointment, the men don't talk to each other. I do a quick two-minute mini dance and the poor kid looks scared of me. He was the big man in front of his friends, but alone, it's like he's never seen a woman.

Just as I'm about to end the dance, I hear one of the guys speaking. "Is there a girl named Sienna that dances here?"

Sienna?

"Times up." I open the curtain for him to leave, and plan to do the same until I hear the guy in the next booth continue talking. My ear stays on the soft cloth as I listen.

"She's my girl and no one fucks with me or my girl." The man stops talking and the curtain moves a moment later, indicating that they're leaving.

I wait a few minutes before I leave the private area and get more drinks. I keep the men with the vests in my peripheral vision at all times. I have a bad feeling about them. It's close to midnight when Robin touches my arm. I've been so focused on the table I didn't notice her.

"Dante's here," she hisses, eyes wide and looking afraid. "You have to leave." She tries to push me toward the exit.

"Trust me, he's not here." I shake my head. Dante would never bring Oakleigh to a place like this. I've seen him with her, he's too protective.

"Trust me, he is. He's in his office." Her hand on my arm tightens and my eyes flick to the hall that leads to his office then back to the table of men I've been watching. They're gone and I see two of them heading out the front door.

"Fine." I fake a smile and Robin lets go of my arm. I walk by her and make my way into the changing room. I grab my bag and toss my work clothes in.

Robin's facial features wash with relief as I head toward the exit but, instead of leaving, I turn the opposite direction and head straight for Dante's office. I'm so angry at him, I can't see straight. He and Oakleigh better not be here.

I push the door in with all of my might. Two men with vests stand over Dante with guns aimed at his head. I frantically look around the room and don't see Oakleigh, but that doesn't mean she's not hiding somewhere. This is the reason why I hid her from Dante in the first place.

The guns swing over to me, giving Dante a moment to get his gun and jump up. Dante shoots one of the guys, and the other guy's gun points back at him.

"None of us are getting out of here alive boys." He's talking to the men of the motorcycle gang.

The one guy is bleeding, but he's alive and raises his gun once more. There are two guns to his one.

"Where is Sienna?" they ask.

My eyes ping-pong back and forth as I'm ignored. If I wasn't so scared, I'd be insulted. I should take a step back and leave but I can't stand here knowing Dante might die. If someone is going to kill him, it will be me.

"I sprayed your mother with the hose today," I interrupt, reminding everyone of my presence.

"Not a good time, Demi," he says, refusing to look at me.

A gun swings toward me. "This your girl? I think it's time for you to know how I'm feeling right now."

A shot is fired, my feet are frozen to the floor and my arm radiates with heat as it's grazed by a bullet. I hiss through the burn. When I look up, both men are dead on the floor and Dante stands, coming toward me.

"What the hell do you think you're doing?" he yells.

"Saving your fucking ass so I can kill you myself when you tell me Oakleigh is hidden in here."

"I would never put her life in danger! You fucking know that!" he hollers back.

"Where the hell is she? You can't leave her by herself."

Dante's arm slips past me and shuts the door to close us in. "She's safe at home with a nanny I hired. I told you I had business to deal with. If I didn't come here..."

"See, this is why I didn't tell you right away." My hands fly through the air. I hit him in his broad chest. Each pound hurts, but he doesn't flinch or make any indication it hurts him.

"Did you really spray my mother with the hose?" The right side of his lips lift upwards in a crooked smirk. It adds to his dangerous handsome look he pulls off.

I snap my fingers. "Focus right now. I'm mad at you."

"We're still trying to run with this, huh?"

"How should I explain to your daughter that the dad she just met got himself killed while he hired a nanny and left her in the middle of the night."

He takes a step toward me and I take a step back. "Good thing you don't have to. You saved me."

"And I got shot for my efforts!"

He looks at my arm. It's red but not bleeding. The bullet grazed me, digging itself into the wall behind.

"To save me."

I roll my eyes. "I did it for our daughter."

"No, you did it because you love me."

I take a step back and meet the wall. "That doesn't matter because I can never change the fact that I didn't tell you about Oakleigh right away."

"Did you really write a hundred letters to her and tell her about me in each one?" he asks.

I tilt my head, confused by his question. I did write her letters, but that was so long ago, and they disappeared one day without a trace.

"Oakleigh showed me all of them tonight."

"What?" I lost those five years ago. There's no way it was Oakleigh...

"Babe," he tilts my chin toward him, so he can look me in the eyes. "She also showed me all the mementos you kept of us. You never wore the bracelet after I gave it to you. I thought you pawned it. I saw the two hundred dollars cash, with your eighteenth-birthday date written on each bill. I'm ready to forgive you. I'm tired of feeling like my heart has been ripped out. I'm sick of missing you."

What is there to say? My eyes dart to the floor and the dead bodies. A normal life would be boring as hell...

"Are you still mad at me for thinking I allowed Oakleigh to be at a strip club?" he fucking chuckles as he asks.

"Yes, I'm mad! Because I know you again, and you're just as perfect as you were back then." I sigh out. "I can't stop loving you, no matter how hard I try, and every time I think about how I broke your trust; it makes me sick."

"Because you love me," he probes.

I hate that he makes me repeat it. It hurts every time I think about how much I love him.

"Yes! Because I love you, you stupid idiot!"

"Good, because I still fucking love you. I can't fucking sleep knowing you're away from me." He crushes his lips to mine.

"Are you sure those guys are dead?" I ask between kisses.

"Want me to shoot them again?"

My shirt is over my head in an instant and I'm tearing at his dress shirt. Buttons go flying and I shove the stiff material over his shoulders and off.

"Shouldn't you be doing something with their bodies?"

"Later. They're not important right now, you are."

Dante pulls at my belt, moving me closer to him as he pulls the leather from around my hips, giving it a snap at the end. My hands are pulling at his dress pants, fumbling with his belt. He helps me before he slips his pants down, his erection bobbing between us. My pants are torn down and I'm lifted up, his cock entering me without warning.

"You have always been mine. I have never stopped loving you. The only way I could stay mad at you was if I was dead."

Dante fucks me hard against the wall. I cling to him, loving the way he feels under my hands. "You will never lie to me again," he demands as he thrusts into me.

He kisses my shoulder and takes my nipple into his mouth. I'm a goner. I cry out his name and he growls mine as we come together.

Slowly, he lets me down and my toes hit the floor as his dick slips out of me. His hand squeezes my breast before slipping down my stomach. I watch with fascination as his hand moves down until he cups my sex. His cum coats my thighs and he uses his fingers to move it back into my pussy.

"I want more children with you. There's nothing hotter than seeing you with my cum in you. You're the first person who has ever made my heart race. I loved you before I even knew what that should feel like. And now, you have blessed me with a daughter. I can't wait to see your belly swollen with our child. I love you with all of my heart, Demi, and I'll never stop."

"I love you too."

"You're sleeping in my bed tonight," Dante cockily states, refusing to ask me. I wait for that feeling to fight him on it but it never comes.

"I like that idea." I shyly smile.

"You're not going back to your mother's house," he adds and I stop. "You sprayed my mother with the hose, she will never forgive you and I want you close to me. Will you please move in with me?"

"Dante."

He gets on one knee. "Demi, please move in with me. I'm a desperate man on his knees begging you."

"Get up." I try to pull him onto his feet. "I'll move in, if you marry me," I say, watching his expression morph into a sexy beast of a grin.

He jumps up from his knees in a sexy ninja move and pulls me in. "Don't mess with me," he warns.

"I love you, Dante. You're the only person to ever make me happy. I want to spend the rest of my days making you happy."

"Fuck yes, Dem!" He kisses me.

There's a knock on his door. "Cleaning crew," is announced from the other side.

Dante places his suit jacket around my upper body before we put our pants back on.

He winks and I look back at the dead guys on the floor before he opens the door, allowing the men in, and takes my hand. "Let's go home."

"Wait! There were more than three of them. They're outside," I explain, concerned.

"Not anymore. They're gone. I promise."

Chapter 39

Dante

I walk into our bedroom after reading Oakleigh a goodnight story. Having that one-on-one time is one of my favorite things to do with her.

"Demi?" I look around our room, not seeing her. A flickering reflection in the window catches my attention and I step closer so I can look out the glass; to see she's gazing at the stars from the roof with a single tealight candle beside her. I lift the wooden frame, ducking my head out. "You know that candle could burn this house down."

She smiles and blows it out. "I was just using it as a beacon for you."

I crawl out and we sit like we used to. She leans into my side, sighing contentedly. "The house sold." The one thing her mother did right was pay off that house. I grunt and hold her tighter.

"The money will help pay for the rest of my schooling."

I kiss the top of her head. "As long as you're happy then I'm happy, but you know money means nothing to me. I wish you would accept my help."

She turns to me. "I am, as much as I can. You pay for everything but my courses."

"Are you happy?" I ask.

She tilts her head up toward mine, her eyes shining with emotion, and gives me that heartbreaking smile of hers.

"Happiest I have ever been."

I sigh with relief. "Me too."

We both look up into the night sky, seeing the same stars we did when we were young. We've come full circle. "I love you," I tell her, never being able to say those words enough.

"I love you more." Her body leans into me, relaxed and content.

My hand slips into my pocket and I bring out a diamond ring. "I know it's not the same one, but it's one of a kind, like you. Demi, will you please wear my ring and be my wife?"

Her hands shake as I slip the ring onto her slender finger.

"Yes, yes!" she wraps her arms around kissing the Hell out of me.

"I want to marry you tomorrow, because I plan to put a baby into that sweet stomach tonight, or as soon as I can."

"What happened to you not wanting to bring children into a world like ours?"

"Babe, all I care about is you by my side. Kids would be a bonus to the arrangement."

Demi

Dressed in the most perfect soft white material, I look at my reflection in the mirror. My hands slide down my hips as I admire my wedding dress. It was over-the-top expensive, and I refused to even consider it, but then it showed up in my closet anyway. Dante assures me he has no idea what it looks like. He told the bridal shop that they were to make sure I walked out of there with the dress of my dreams.

The neckline is a semi sweetheart, leaving my shoulders bare. The material is snug at my waist before it flows out. My hair rests in curls over my right shoulder, gathered in a simple, low ponytail.

"Dad is going to pick you up and walk you right out of the church when he sees how beautiful you look," Oakleigh says in awe as she stares at my reflection too.

Turning around, a wave of emotions overwhelms me. I never thought I'd ever get married at all, and here I am getting ready to marry the man of my dreams.

Oakleigh hugs me. "I stole the church keys. I plan to lock the doors the moment you step onto the red carpet so dad can't steal you away from everyone."

I hold her back, chuckling at how much she can be like Dante. "You ready?" I ask.

My stomach flutters with excitement as Oakleigh opens the door for us and we step out of the small bridal room. Soft music floats out of the main room. Oakleigh pulls a key out of the pocket of her dress and locks the door just like she said she would. "Do you want to keep the key or should I?" she asks.

"I'll let you do the honors."

We nod to the man waiting to open the doors for us. Oakleigh goes first and I wait for my song. When it comes on, I take a deep breath. Holding my flowers with both hands, I step from behind the door to the middle of the doorway. Everyone is already standing.

My eyes drift immediately to Dante. He looks stunning in a suit at the end of the aisle. I step in and take a few steps. Dante is already walking down the red carpet. Instead of lifting me over his shoulders like a barbarian and running outside, he loops his arms around mine and walks with me down the aisle.

He gives me a soft peck on the lips before stepping into place in front of the wedding officiant. "You are breathtaking, Demi. It's taking all of my will power not to take you into a back room and show you what you do to me." My neck heats and it makes its way into my cheeks. "Your blushing is making my cock harder for you."

The man performing our ceremony clears his throat and Dante steps back, keeping my hands in his.

We repeat our vows, one after another. We're not even pronounced husband and wife when Dante sweeps me into his arms and kisses me. In the background I hear our ceremony concluded as Dante's family cheers and claps. Soon, his brother Romeo begins to yell that there are children in the crowd, and only then does Dante let go of me.

He rights me on my feet, giving me a wink.

We walk down the aisle as husband and wife, the thought still surreal to me that Dante is mine forever now. Everything is how it should be. For once, I get my happy ending, and the wait only made our ending sweeter and more precious.

Chapter 40

Epilogue

2 years later

"I have the ID, passport, and an apartment rented under the new names," I announce. All the new 'documents' are laid out on the counter of our kitchen while I admire them. My hand rests on my flat stomach.

Dante ignores my comments, walking right toward me and kissing me. "I love it when you talk dirty to me," he teases. "It makes me want to put a baby in you."

"Oakleigh is in the other room," I protest in a hushed voice.

"Doesn't mean I want to fuck you any less." He kisses my neck, tickling me, and I giggle.

"Stop making out, I'm coming in!" Oakleigh hollers, happily.

I nudge Dante away and he concedes because our daughter is in the room.

"For the record"—she opens the fridge, looks in it, then shuts it, facing us—"I would love to be a big sister to three or four siblings." She has the freezer open now, looking around.

"See? She's on my side," Dante gloats, whispering into my ear.

"We have nothing good to eat," our daughter complains, before rummaging in the cupboard. Our kitchen is packed with food. Two years ago, she would have never said such a thing.

"I can always find something to eat," Dante whispers into my ear. "In fact, I think I want my dessert right now."

"Gross!" Oakleigh throws a tea towel at us. "I can hear you!"

Dante clears his throat and goes into the freezer. "What? I want ice cream," he says innocently.

Now he has Oakleigh's full attention and she turns back facing us. "I haven't had breakfast yet," she replies hesitantly.

"Neither have I." He smiles, grabbing two bowls down.

"Might as well, make me a bowl too," I announce, and Oakleigh grabs another bowl. "Because I'm eating for two now."

The bowl crashes to the floor and I'm instantly being hugged by both of them. "Don't play with me Demi," Dante growls, placing his hand on my stomach.

"I've taken five tests to make sure. We're having a baby!"

"That's why you didn't argue with me when I said going to get those girls would be too risky for you this time." His eyes light with awareness. I have been helping Dante free women from the trafficking ring but this time I allowed him to convince me to help with the paperwork instead.

"You sneaky little wife." He leans into my ear. "I'm going to have to punish you for that later."

"And here I thought I was being a good girl," I tease, nibbling on his ear.

"I'm still here in the room," Oakleigh calls. "Why do I have to have such weird parents?" she mumbles under her breath but her smile stays firmly planted on her face. She loves seeing us happy.

"Mom and I had an idea." Our attention moves to our daughter. I did tell her to ask when Dante was in a good mood to leave no room for him to say no.

"I want to create our own 'documents' instead of outsourcing. I've shown Mom what I can do and, with some classes and practice, I could be as good as or better than the guy you use currently."

Dante glances at me. "You and your mom think, huh?"

"Might as well keep the business in the family, right?" I innocently bat my eyes at him.

"I think it's a great idea." Dante confirms.

Oakleigh jumps up and down, clapping her hands. "Mom was so certain you'd say no, but I knew better."

She comes up and gives us both another hug. Everything I have ever wanted, I now have. Sometimes I have to pinch myself to make sure I'm not dreaming. Dante presses a kiss to the top of my head. "I love you, Demi."

I squeeze him with my arm wrapped around his waist. "Looks like we get our happily ever after ending, after all."

Want to know what happens to Sienna? Her and Max's story is in Throne of Obsession, releasing this year!

Did you know that Savio has a book? Read Throne of Diamonds.

Chapter 41

Acknowledgments

THANK YOU SO MUCH for reading Throne of Sin. If you can do me a favor, can you please leave a review. Reviews are so important for authors.

I hope you loved Dante and Demi as much as I do! I loved their darkness and how their being together helped heal each other.

My **beta readers** take my unpolished words and help to create the story better. Linda, Chanel and Krista I appreciate you so much.

David my editor, thank you for always working so hard on my edits. You're input helps make a smoother read.

Karina my proof reader you are always willing to work with a quick deadline. I appreciate you so much. Thank you for everything you do. The teasers you create are beautiful.

Juliana at jersey girl design, your book covers are always amazing. You take my ideas and create something so special. Thank you.

Give me books thank you for organizing my cover reveal and release. A huge thank you to all readers and bloggers who have helped me along the way.

Chapter 42

Other books by Emily Bowie

DARK MAFIA SINS SERIES (Romantic Suspense / Mafia)

Sinful Vow: (Luca & Aly) kidnapping, forced marriage
Sinful Daughter : (Aria & Theo) enemies to lovers, mafia princess/cop,
Sinful Kisses: (Gia & Romeo) enemies to lovers
Sinful Bodyguard: (Fin and Luna) A mafia bodyguard romance
Sinful Queen : (Katrina and Demetri) A secret baby, mafia romance
Each book can be read as a standalone

Mafia Thrones

Throne of Diamonds: (Savio & Charlotte) arranged marriage, strong female lead romance
Throne of Sin: (Dante & Demi) second chance romance
Throne of Obsession: (Max & Sienna) Stalker, mafia romance coming this 2023
Each book can be read as a standalone

Oakport Beach Series (Small Beach Town / Romantic Comedy)

Crashing Heart (Crash & Piper's story) Summer fling/ falling for your boss romance

Southern Hearts (Danger & Haven's story) Friends to Lovers romance

Wild Hearts (Frankie & Deacon's story) enemies to lovers

*each of these books is a standalone and can be read in any order.

Steele Family Series (Small Town / Romantic Suspense)

Stolen Moments (book #1) (Shay & Luke) Brother's best friend romance

Moonlight Moments (Book #2) (Kellen & Sloan) Insta love (fling to forever)

Bittersweet Moments (book #3) (Brax & Raya) Secret baby

Whisky Moments (book #4) (Rhett & Camilla) Enemies to lovers, Rock star romance

All books are designed to be read as a standalone. Although, characters do have a reoccurring role in each book.

Box set of the Steele Family series:

Standalones: (Small Town / Romantic Suspense)

Pretty, Twisted Lies (Kiptyn's book):

Kiptyn McGrath:

Kellie Dare was never meant to be mine. We existed in two different worlds. Mine was dark, dangerous, and unpredictable. Her's held prestige, wealth, and promise. I was never her white knight but allowed her to believe it until the day she forgot she was mine. I quickly became the villain who would stop at nothing to keep her.

Bennett Brothers Series (Small Town/Romantic Suspense)

Recklessly mine (book #1) second chance love

Recklessly Forbidden (book #2) small town romance

Recklessly Devoted (book #3) enemies to lovers, next-door neighbors

Box set of the Bennett Brothers:

Made in United States
Orlando, FL
14 February 2024

43666841R00146